THE DEVIL'S DEBT

BLOOD SPLATTER BOOKS

RICK WOOD

ALSO BY RICK WOOD

Blood Splatter Books
Psycho B*tches
Shutter House
This Book is Full of Bodies
Home Invasion
Haunted House
Woman Scorned
This Book is Full of More Bodies
He Eats Children
The Devil's Debt
Perverted Little Freak

Cia Rose
When the World Has Ended
When the End Has Begun
When the Living Have Lost
When the Dead Have Decayed

The Edward King Series
I Have the Sight
Descendant of Hell
An Exorcist Possessed
Blood of Hope
The World Ends Tonight

Anthologies
Twelve Days of Christmas Horror
Twelve Days of Christmas Horror Volume 2
Twelve Days of Christmas Horror Volume 3
Roses Are Red So Is Your Blood

Standalones

When Liberty Dies

The Death Club

Chronicles of the Infected

Zombie Attack

Zombie Defence

Zombie World

Non-Fiction

How to Write an Awesome Novel

Horror, Demons and Philosophy

One of the artifices of Satan is to induce men to believe that he does not exist: another, perhaps equally fatal, is to make them fancy that he is obliged to stand quietly by, and not to meddle with them, if they get into true silence.

- John Wilkinson, 1836

THE DEBT

ONE

To say that Brian was a modest, humble man was like saying that a giraffe was short, or that politicians were fair, or that a neo-Nazi was a well-rounded individual that contributed well to the community.

He was a self-involved, self-infatuated, self-obsessed, self-aggrandised, self-centred, contrite, insincere, vainglorious mess who cared little for what an individual thought of him, but cared greatly for the opinions of the online masses.

He had 489 followers on Instagram.

679 followers on Twitter.

856 followers on Facebook.

But, should you ask him how many followers he has, do not expect him to answer with these figures. In fact, do not expect him to quote you any figures—instead, expect him to use lots of words that avoid quoting such figures, but still inflate and distort his apparently grand following in a way that makes him seem hugely successful.

And when he gives you this grand impression of himself,

he is not lying—not because he is telling the truth, but because you can't be lying if you actually believe what you are saying.

Brian's mother, father and sister all left the house at eight in the morning and returned at six in the evening, spending all day at jobs they hated, all so they could pay the mortgage and have food in the fridge.

But not Brian.

Oh, not Brian.

Brian lived under the deluded belief that he was waiting for fame and was too important to sink himself to such trivialities. Being an influencer was his calling, and any time his family nagged him, he would just tell them they didn't understand. But, in reality, Brian was a bum who hated the idea of having a proper job. He was desperate to be rich, but unwilling to commit to hard work; so much so that he would fall for any clickbait he saw on the internet that claimed he could earn big money and earn it quickly. He'd lost weeks of dole money on get-rich quick solitaire games, on poorly advised stock investments, and on bitcoin exchanges. He'd spent an entire overdraft on pointless courses from *real* influencers that claimed they could teach him to be as successful as them, only to find that their methods did not work. And he'd maxed out two credit cards on paying for more Instagram followers, just to find that the fake accounts unfollowed him a month later.

And why did he keep trying these things when they were obviously cons?

Because his determination was greater than his stupidity. He would try anything that carried the possibility of giving his existence some semblance of meaning; anything that would match reality to the inflated self-perception he so stubbornly believed in.

And he lied to others as much as he lied to himself.

When he played Call of Duty every evening, he would tell his online opponents that he was a big name, and they should be respectful. When he received abusive comments online—as tends to happen in the toxic culture of social media—he would engage in a heated back and forth of abusive words designed to offend any characteristic the other person may have to alleviate any feeling that he had been beaten. And when he walked through town, he would wear baggy jeans and keep his hood up, scowling at those who passed him in a poor attempt at being intimidating.

But honestly, he was a nobody.

Less than a nobody.

He grew up as a scrawny middle-class kid who'd never had an actual fight, was too obnoxious to retain friends, and rarely found himself on the guest list to any party. He spoke down to others, mocked their insecurities, and laughed at anyone who struggled at something new. He would interrupt people's stories to tell them about his own accomplishments, then stare at them in anticipation of praise. He'd kill conversations by interjecting comments about his own brilliance, then wonder why people never asked him to embellish.

He never smiled in photos. Always applied the dark filter to his selfies. Often used hashtags such as #RealLife #JustSaying and #DontGetOffendedGrandma. And he blocked anyone who had the audacity to call him out on his attention-seeking posts.

He had a good family, too—his parents were perfect examples of how two people should love each other; his little sister had been Head Girl at their senior school before going to university and graduating with first-class honours; and his white privileged suburban upbringing provided him with every Christmas present he ever asked for, every resource he needed for school, and funding for further education should he ever wake up one day with a sudden change of attitude, like Scrooge in the final stave of A Christmas Carol, eager to do something better with his life. But even the Ghosts of Christmas Past, Present or Future wouldn't bother with him. It would be a waste of time. It's hard to teach someone to be less self-involved when they were too self-involved to listen to you.

To Brian, there was one person who mattered, and one person who was badass, and one person who deserved respect for not having accomplished anything, and it was *him*.

Still, there was the niggling voice at the back of his head that told him that, one day, he'd have to wake up and realise he didn't have the online following or adoration he believed he had. But alas, those who are this deluded don't tend to acknowledge such sensical voices. They were a hinderance; a stumbling block; a minor thought that could not penetrate his armour of arrogance.

Brian would not be told anything by anybody, and that was how he was.

And when someone refuses to listen, that means you need to teach them another way.

Which brings us to Christmas Eve, several years before the events of this story unfold. His parents had invited his family around, and his sister, aunts, uncles and cousins had shown up ready for games of charades and present exchanges. Brian, however, shut himself in the darkness of his room, engrossed in another game on the Xbox, preferring to argue over his headset with strangers than spend the festive season with the few people willing to dote a little love upon him. That was, until his mother knocked on the door and, not receiving a response, proceeded into the room.

Brian didn't turn around, not wishing to witness his mother's dismay at the plates with pizza crusts on the floor, the mass of stained cups on the windowsill, and the aroma that Brian couldn't place. He was twenty-three, and an adult, and therefore not interested in the irritating commands of his mother—commands that, whilst being irritating, evidently weren't irritating enough for him to a get a job and move out.

(Of course, Brian would purport that being an influencer was his job—but the issue with this is that, for something to be a job, one must make money out of it.)

"Brian, your family is here," she told the back of his head. "They'd love to see you."

Brian threw a grenade and ran. He hid, blew up another person, then listened to them shouting abuse at him through his headset.

"Brian!"

Noticing his mother's reflection in the screen, Brian told the group of strangers that he would be a moment, rotated his head, and offered her a grunt of, "What?"

"I said your family is here."

Brian shrugged.

"Everyone's waiting to see you."

"So?"

"Do I need to turn the electricity off like last year?"

"Fine!" He exited the game and threw his controller across the room, and it landed on the cushion of his duvet—he wished to make a stand, but he didn't want to break his controller.

"Is that what you're wearing?" his mother asked, looking at his t-shirt. There was a bogie crust on his collar, and the text read *You find it offensive? I don't, and that's why I'm happier than you.*

"God, Mum, leave me alone!" He sounded just as petulant in his early twenties as he did in his adolescence, and his mum would express her disappointment in him if she thought it would make a difference.

Brian stomped down the stairs. He barged into the room of merriment, the lights on the Christmas tree tacky and flashing, and everyone greeted him. He folded his arms, put up his hood, and offered an intelligible grunt. His legs ached after a few minutes of standing—sitting on his arse all day hadn't made him particularly fit—and he waited for someone to get up. Eventually, his Great Aunt Meredith needed to go to the other room to change her catheter bag. He took her seat, deciding that he would be unwilling to give it back should she wish to reacquire it.

"Oh, Brian," his mother said, entering the room with an empty milk carton. "We're out of milk. Would you mind popping to the shops to get another?"

He rolled his eyes, huffed, and stretched his head back. "I already came downstairs, isn't that enough?"

"I'll give you some money for you to get your gaming magazine as well."

He considered the proposition and, after a few seconds, decided that a few minutes' walk to retrieve some milk would be worth the reward of his magazine. It had a review of a new zombie game in that was all the rage, and he was eager to read the magazine's verdict. So he took the money, put on his shoes, put on his coat (on his mother's insistence), and left the house for the chilly breeze and icy pavement.

And that, my friends, is where I met Brian, and where his life changed. Whether for worse or for better, I will let you decide—I, myself, am looking forward to it.

It's going to be hugely entertaining.

CHAPTER

TWO

Brian stomped out of his house, crunched across the snow, then knocked into the lamppost as he turned down the street—a lamppost he immediately squared up to, scowling as if it had just started a fight with him. Fortunately for Brian, a lamppost cannot fight back, so he could count this as a victory.

He pulled his hood over his head, shoved his hands in his pockets, and marched down the street with the misguided belief that the hood gave him the appearance of a cool and intimidating figure, rather than like the baby animal he more closely resembled.

This time of the year meant little to Brian. Not anymore, anyway. As a child, he was an avid believer in Santa Claus, and insisted until the age of twelve that they left a glass of sherry and a mince pie out for the festive toy dealer. Even after he learned that he had been lied to throughout his entire childhood—brainwashed, even, into believing an omnipotent obese old man snuck into his room with honourable gift-giving intentions—he continued the charade for his younger sister far into his teenage years. It's hard to say at what point he became spoilt, cynical, and rude. Perhaps he became a grumpy teenager and never grew out of it. Perhaps years of bullying had left him with a thick skin portrayed as self-assurance. Perhaps he'd always had everything he ever wanted, so never had the opportunity to learn lessons from tough experiences.

Or maybe he was just a dick.

Either way, he didn't care. What did it matter what anyone else thought of him?

Once he'd left his street, he trudged around the corner and passed a park where a group of children paused their snowball fight to let him pass, for which he did not thank them. He turned another corner and made brief eye contact with an old lady, and she glanced away as she passed him. It gave him a tremble of excitement to think that he had the power to frighten another person, and he replayed the moment in his mind.

As he approached the off licence, he took his phone from his pocket and filmed the entrance. He uploaded the five-second footage to social media with the following text over-layed: When parents need you to go get their shit from the store #FuckChristmas #FuckParents #FuckAids.

(Don't ask why the last hashtag was present—I'm not sure Brian could even explain it.)

He entered the store, grimacing at the sound of the doorbell announcing his entry, and felt the eyes of a middle-aged Asian man behind the counter follow him as he walked up one aisle and down another. He grumbled at the attention. He didn't intend to steal anything. He wasn't an actual criminal, he just wanted to look like one. Still, it gave him something to moan about online later.

He collected the four-pint carton of semi-skimmed milk, handed the change to the man behind the counter, then traipsed out of the store. He could not put both hands in his pockets because he needed one to carry the milk, which annoyed him as it ruined his 'image.' To him, any moment outside was a moment to maintain what he hoped was a hostile presence. His grumpiness was his USP as far as he was concerned—his 'unique selling point' for those of you who, unlike Brian, do not need to shorten every phrase into an acronym to save the second spent on extra syllables— and he believed it was why people followed him on social media.

Except, people didn't really want to follow him on social media. Despite his belief that he was an influencer, the only thing he ever really influenced was the quantity of porn on his computer.

Meanwhile, some actual scary-looking men crossed the road toward him—blokes with muscles and jewellery who, unlike Brian, didn't look like infant monkeys with their hoods up. They were nudging each other and being generally rowdy. Frightened by the sight, Brian's body shrunk in on itself and he turned away. He pulled his hood down further to conceal his face and aimed himself the other way across the road.

Unfortunately, that hood didn't only conceal his face from the group of men who'd sparked a feeling of fear in his gut—it also concealed Brian's eyes from the bus that was driving toward him at exactly thirty-six miles per hour.

The pain of impact was so excruciating that, when he landed seconds later, the agony had already stolen his consciousness from him. The force of the bus had shattered his spine, and the collision of his skull against frozen cement rendered his brain useless.

A crowd gathered around him, and those men he'd interpreted as thugs dialled 999 and urged the ambulance to hurry. A pool of blood crept across the road, ending as the snow thickened, and his contorted, misshapen body lay on the road, lit by the hazard lights of a nearby car, delivering trauma to those who witnessed the sight.

He wasn't breathing. His heart wasn't beating. His blood wasn't flowing.

Basically, in short, the fucker was dead.

THREE

This is where I came in.

I sat back in my chair, the arms of which were decadent and grand, decorated in red jewels and screaming faces; the back of which spiralled toward the ceiling, sculpted out of stone; and the bottom of which was built on many, many skulls of many, many tyrants. The walls were crimson, and the ground was blood-red gravel. The fire place, black and grand, was home to an enormous set of flames over bones and firewood. It felt hot, but everywhere in Hell is hot—it's built on volcanos and lava and fire pits, what do you expect?

I chuckled at the sight of Brian looking small and slight opposite me. His chair appeared pathetic opposite my extravagant throne; it was small, made of weak wood, and every movement prompted a creak; the back was cracked and dug into his bony back, and the bumps of the seat meant he was permanently wriggling—whilst mine had leather padding over the skulls of the damned.

His eyes widened at the sight of me, and he tried to get

up, but found himself unable. It made me chuckle to see him unable to stand, and to be so confused as to why. He even screamed a little, as is to be expected—The Devil is quite a hideous sight to a human's fallible perception.

And let's be absolutely clear—a human's perception of the world is incredibly fallible. None of you know anything. Honestly, it truly amazes me how enlightened humans think they are. You must understand—I know *all* the answers to *all* the questions you keep asking about your meek existence. And do you know what makes it worse? These answers are *all* right in front of you, yet you will never see them; your arrogance makes you unable to comprehend what is so easily comprehensible. If you had any idea how little you actually knew, you'd be astounded at how thick you all actually are.

Eventually, Brian stopped struggling, and the shock turned into anger. He scowled at me, which made me chuckle more, and his scowl intensified, and my chuckles turned into guffaws which turned into hysterics. He was trying to intimidate me, with absolutely no idea who I was. It's rather amusing, isn't it?

"What's going on?" he demanded.

"Why ever do you quibble so much, boy? You ought to sit back and relax. We have all the time in the world."

It was true. We could have sat there for years, but the moment our conversation ended and he returned to his mortal confines (if I should choose to allow him to), merely half a second would have passed. The concept of time is yet another thing humans made up to explain what they don't understand.

"Why can't I get up? Fucking knock it off!"

I laughed again. "Your cursing won't offend me like it

13

offends your ever suffering mother, you reclusive urchin. Curse away for your heart's desire should you wish, I couldn't give a damn."

I reached over to the coffee table beside me—sculpted out of the faces of shrieking youths—then opened a tin and took out a Turkish delight wrapped in red foil. I unwrapped it as noisily as I could, placed the sweet on the tip of my tongue, took it into my mouth, and chewed loudly as I sat back and crossed my legs. I wanted Brian to know how much I enjoyed my treat.

"What is this?" He looked around. "Where am I?"

The bit where they struggle to come to terms with where they are always takes a while, so I'll skip the formalities with you. It's my least favourite part—there isn't a man, woman or ungendered soul who hasn't sat here and rejected the notion of where they are, once again demonstrating the human's inability to correctly perceive what is around them. It usually starts with denial—"This isn't Hell you aren't real stop it"—then anger—"How dare you, let me go, I will not be kept prisoner"—followed by bargaining—"If you let me go I will make it worth your while"—a smattering of depression—"I can't believe I'm actually dead, this is horrible"—followed, ever so exquisitely, by acceptance—"Well, what do you want then?"

Brian, in his volatile state and detestable manner, took exceptionally long to come to this stage, and I had made it through almost the whole tin of Turkish delights before he finally reached a point where I could reason with him—as much as a fool such as this can be reasoned with, anyway.

Finally, he looked me up and down, scanning my Dolce Gabbana suit (What? The Devil likes class!); my blood-red skin; my large, curved claws; my slashing tail; then raised his gaze to my horned head.

"Who the fuck are you?" he asked, with a tone of entitlement I was struggling to tolerate, despite how common such a trait is in those who usually frequent his chair.

"My dear, who do you think I am?"

I clicked my fingers, and a glass of Agua del Diablo appeared in my claws. I took a sip and relished the sharp sting against the back of my throat—I will admit, despite how ridiculous most human creations are, I do appreciate the invention of whisky.

"Why can't I move?"

"Because I don't want you to move. Silly boy..."

"I don't understand."

"What a surprise."

I took another sip, feeling the fire fall through me, and placed the glass on the coffee table.

"Are you ready to stop moaning yet?" I asked. "You can continue if you want. I'm in no rush, but it is rather delaying the inevitable, don't you think?"

"The inevitable?"

"Yes—the offer you will say yes to."

"I ain't saying yes to nothing you offer."

I tutted. "Gosh, such poor diction, such abuse of your native language. Do you do that on purpose, my child? Do you speak like that to disguise your upper-middle class upbringing? Because I have no doubt your mother did not teach you such vernacular."

"What are you on about?"

"Yes. You're right. Let's get to it—no time like the present." I uncrossed my legs and leant toward my guest. "I have an offer for you."

"An offer? I don't want anything you have to offer."

"That's what they usually say before they realise they are dead."

"Dead?"

"Yes. Dead, you ingrate. Dead all over."

"I am not dead."

"Not dead? My boy, where do you think you are?"

He frowned, and went to object, but didn't. Instead, he turned his head and listened. Shouts and screams created a distant symphony; the wails of the damned were a joyous melody from afar. He could see the volcanos rising into the fiery sky behind me; the pits of lava spewing over nearby rocks; flying beasts freely filling the air.

"Holy fucking shit," he gasped.

"Yes, that is right, my dear boy, let the realisation overcome you, let your understanding finally settle in, let your mind become clear with the truth—you, you ungrateful cretin, you disgusting little vagabond, are in Hell."

"Hell? But why am I in Hell?"

"Why wouldn't you be? Tell me, what divine right would you have to go to Heaven? What acts of kindness have you bestowed on others that might pave your path to the celestial holy land? No, I have had my claws on your soul for a long time, waiting for this moment, and I am ever so fortunate that it arrived now."

His face turned pale and his eyes filled with tears.

"Wh—wh—what do I do here?" he asked, a tremble in his voice that made me hard in all sorts of ways.

"Why, you are damned for all eternity! You will spend the rest of your never-ending unlife being tortured, molested by claws, shredded of your skin, impaled by swords, burned alive, and torn apart to be put back together and torn apart again."

"B—b—but I... I don't want to be here..."

"Well no one wants to be here, my dear. No human, anyway. Demons bloody love it."

"Please—please help me—please don't make me stay."

"Don't make you stay? Why, my child, my subject, my muse—you belong nowhere else. Your mortal world would not have you back, would they? You have come here for a reason. No, you are here, and we best start your torture straight away. Just tell me"—I leant forward and looked deep into his pathetic, terrified little eyes—"in which orifice would you like the sharp, red-hot fire stick first?"

Tears danced down his cheeks, leaving snail trails of terror. I wanted to lick them up. They smelt beautiful.

"But... Mum... Dad... My sister... I—I didn't... I didn't mean to..."

"No one means to do anything. No one intends to become a nasty little wretch like you. It just happens, doesn't it?"

He whimpered some more.

"Right, well!" I stood. "Best be going. Let's get started."

I lifted my hand and he rose from the chair, floating behind me, toward the grand, gold gates of Hell that rose above the fires. A rotting sign across the gates read *He Who Hath Entered Shall Never Return*. His crying grew louder at the sight of it; his begging more vigorous; his distress all the more intoxicating.

"No, please, please, I'll do anything! Anything!"

I paused. Turned toward him. Grinned.

"Anything?"

Now there was the word I was waiting for.

"Yes, anything."

I allowed him to return to his chair, where he resettled, and I returned to the chair opposite.

"Now, do you mean that?" I asked. "Because many men say they will do anything, but when it comes to it, they are unwilling to do what I request of them."

"No, I will—I will do anything—*anything*."

"Well, then, if you are sure."

"I am, I am!"

"Okay then. Well, here is the deal I offer you. It is on my terms, and my terms only."

"That's okay, that's fine, please, just anything…"

I took a moment to enjoy his desperation. This has always been, and still is, my favourite part.

"I will restore your life. You will wake up in hospital, uninjured from your unfortunate, life-ending calamity. You will walk again, talk again, and have no injuries—in fact, doctors will say you were a miraculous case—an anomaly— one in a million."

"Oh, yes, please, that would be great, yes, please."

"Do you know what else? I will also throw in seven years of fortune. You will have the best luck known to man. You will succeed and prevail. Your social media with gather followers in their millions, and you will make money you've never imagined making, and the women… oh, the women… how they will fall over you."

"That would be brilliant, thank you, oh thank you…"

"Ah, ah, ah, not so fast. This isn't free. And you said you will do anything."

"Yes, anything. Anything!"

"Then listen closely."

I took a moment. Breathed in his fear. It smelt like freshly mown grass on a summer's day. It was intoxicating.

"After these seven years are up, I will revisit you, and you will repay me. A life for every year you experience success. That will be your debt. Do you understand?"

He said nothing. Quivering. Confused.

"I said, do you understand?"

He stared at me. Then at the gates. At the volcanos. The

lava. The demons. Listening to the screams. Aware of what the alternative was.

But Brian didn't need much coaxing. In fact, he needed none. Other people's lives were but tools for manipulation to a man like Brian. The loss of another life to aid his success was merely a required exchange, and not a burden to bear.

At least, not yet.

"Fine."

In the instant the contract was formed, he awoke.

He was on the ground. Voices were near. Paramedics above him. Shouts of *he's breathing* and *he's still alive* and *get him in the ambulance.*

His eyes shut again, and when they opened again, he was in the hospital, and they were telling him how bizarre his case was. How he shouldn't be alive. How it was something they had never witnessed before.

He held onto the vague memory of his meeting with me for as long as he could convince himself it was real. However, much like many in his situation would do, he put it down to trauma. Vivid hallucinations of a mind under extreme stress. He was fighting for his life, of course he'd see stuff, of course he'd imagine me. Human perception is fallible, remember? People always say they saw bright lights when they were close to death, but that doesn't mean there's an afterlife, it just means you see what you think you are going to see.

And he'd seen... something ridiculous, when he thought about it.

And he thought about it very little over the next week, even as millions of followers started praising his every post, and the advertising deals came in, and the women started messaging him.

It was almost as if it hadn't happened—but, honestly, it

was more than that. He became preoccupied with how magnificent his life had become, and simply stopped giving a fuck.

ALMOST SEVEN YEARS
LATER

CHAPTER
FOUR

I despise so much of what my divine alternative (God) has vomited over this abhorrent world. Cricket, broccoli, extroverts, Americans, the Kardashians—I hate it all with such vigour that often I must stop and calm myself, such is the hatred that fills my immortal body. But there is one thing God has bestowed on the world that I can make good use of.

Vocabulary.

He has given us so many languages with so many words and so many ways of putting things. He has given us adjectives, similes, metaphors, nouns, hyperbole, and I adore every fanciful use of it.

But say that, perhaps, for some reason unknown to myself or you, much of language was abolished, and I had to choose one adjective to describe Brian's new lifestyle – out of all the many words I might retain for such an occasion, the word I would keep in this situation is, without a doubt or a shred of thought needing to be given: lavish.

His life had become *lavish*.

Lavish house with shiny clean windows and lavish

doors with fancy architecture and a lavish garden with a gigantic swimming pool and a lavish interior with so many rooms he didn't have use for all of them. Lavish tastes in expensive champagne and luxurious aperitifs and fancy meals made by world-renowned chefs; lavish women with fake fingernails and fake eyelashes with weak intelligence and an even weaker ability to say no; and lavish arrivals at family gatherings in Ferraris and an unnecessary *fuck you* attitude. Everything, all the time, without fail, lavish, lavish, lavish.

He was not humble before, but one could at least relate to his misery. Now, no one could relate to his tumultuous moods, and no one could understand how a man who had so much wealth could be the slightest bit miserable, but despondency was his permanent state. His happiness came from his perpetual moodiness; there was nothing more appealing to him than generating sympathy from those who would otherwise not care.

His career as an influencer—if that is what such cretins call a career nowadays—had gone from remarkable strength to remarkable highs. There were few advertisers who weren't willing to give him the better parts of their budgets for him to simply hold their drink in one of his videos, or to eat their product in a photo, or to wear their jacket at influencer award parties.

But what were his videos actually about?

Be fucked if I knew.

There was no real branding. No real consistency. No real reason anyone would enjoy such pointless, endless videos.

In fact, someone made this observation, frequently posting the same comment, over and over, on video after video: *boring af.* Not particularly offensive, but enough to compel Brian to post a screenshot of this person's username on his social media—an act that meant the poor boy was inundated with vile messages—and to pay a private investigator to find out where this stranger worked. He released this information and encouraged his followers to go in and complain about the troll's conduct. Brian even allowed himself a slight smile when this troll messaged him to complain that he'd been fired due to all the customer complaints made against him. It was what the little prick deserved.

And the fame! Brian would often walk from his house to the park, or a restaurant, or another date, and would be recognised, with some random nomad eager to tell him how much they loved him, and how great his videos were. Despite the smugness it prompted inside of him, he would give them only a small obligatory thanks, take a photo with them, then walk away with his unfailing arrogance clearly apparent.

And have I got onto the women yet?

Oh, the women! How they flocked toward him!

Not good women, as such—if I am permitted to say such a thing (I know it sounds highly judgemental). By this I mean they were not women one would bring home to their mothers, nor were they women one might engage in a prolonged and deep discussion, and nor were they women a man might seek for intimate, long-term happiness. They were the kind of women some men used as trophies—women men used to brag to other men about their conquests.

He rarely satisfied any of these women. He let them perform their own foreplay and told them they were privileged to suck his cock, then fucked them until he came at an average of one minute or less. What was the point in caring about their pleasure? If he was not to see them again, then what they took out of the encounter was not worth his consideration. They were only there to please him.

In fact, that was how he saw the entire world. Everyone was here to either suck his figurative dick or get out of his way.

And that night, almost seven years ago, when he died briefly and woke up with a miraculous recovery—for what little reality of it exists in his memory—was something that rarely crossed his mind.

Did it really happen?

Probably not.

More likely, it was the hallucination of a traumatised mind; the delusion of near death anxiety. It was from his unconscious, or wherever his mind might store such nonsense.

Although, with the anniversary approaching, the encounter was surfacing in his thoughts more frequently, occasionally finding his mind drifting back to the deal he made with the imaginary devil, and what might happen if it were true.

The doctors had told him they were astounded that he not only survived, but could walk and talk as he did before the accident. His recovery defied expectation or explanation. So what if, maybe, possibly, the deal was real? What if The Devil was to arrive and collect his debt?

Nonsense.

Rubbish.

A load of shit.

Not even worth thinking about.

Yet, as he approached his sister's house on the day before Christmas Eve—a house vastly inferior to his with a few child's toys covered in snow on the lawn—he paused.

Looked down the street.

And, just for a moment, he thought he saw me watching him. Far away, at the end of the street unlit by lamplight; the end where the shadows lived, where the pavement was shrouded in darkness.

But he didn't see me.

I stayed in the darkness, and I watched him, considering when to appear.

Not yet.

I wanted him to see what he had to lose first.

I wanted him to experience the life I would take away if he failed to fulfil his side of the deal.

I wanted him to see the only person he loved in this world beside himself. I wanted him to experience their presence one last time.

So I let him roll his eyes. Shrug his shoulders. Dismiss what he thought he'd heard.

He entered his sister's house without knocking, much to the fury of her husband, but to the delight of her daughter.

CHAPTER
FIVE

"We have a doorbell you know!"

"I'm sure you do, Mike." Brian barged past his brother-in-law and rushed into the living room, where he found his niece, Lily, beside the Christmas tree, reading a book about a caterpillar with an immense craving for food.

"Uncle Brian!" she declared, and immediately opened her arms as wide as she could to receive his hug. He wrapped his arms around her and lifted her from the floor, spinning her, laughing as she giggled.

"And how are you?" Brian asked. "Are you excited for Christmas?"

"Yes! I asked Santa for a new bike."

"Did you?"

"And we spoke about that, didn't we?" Mike said, appearing in the doorway. "About how the cost of living is making Santa a little hard up, and that he might not bring her a bike this year."

With a grin, Brian said, "Oh, I'm sure that's nonsense.

The cost of living at the North Pole is as same as it always is—Santa will have no problem bringing your bike."

"You really think so, Uncle Brian?"

Mike huffed, rolled his eyes, and stomped out of the room. Brian couldn't help but allow himself a sneaky smile as he settled Lily on the floor and picked up the book she had been reading.

"What's this?"

"It's my book."

"The Hungry Caterpillar—and just how hungry is this caterpillar?"

"*Very* hungry!"

"Hi, Brian," said Clarissa, appearing in the doorway.

"Hey, little sister."

"You know, if you want to keep coming here, you must get on with Mike."

"Oh, I'm sure that's not true."

Brian despised Mike.

Albeit, Brian despised most people who were not himself, but he despised Mike especially. Clarissa met Mike in the days following Brian's accident; he had been kept in the hospital for a few days because the doctors could not accept that there could be nothing wrong with him after such a terrible accident. Not only did the boredom perturb Brian, but he was also increasingly perturbed by his sister; she was supposed to be visiting him, but spent more time flirting with another patient, Mike. She was meant to be there to give Brian attention, and there was little that riled Brian more than not being given the attention he felt he deserved.

Besides, his little sister was in his life before she was in Mike's. He was more entitled to her love than he was.

"Would you like to read any other books?"

"Yeah! Will you do the voices again?"

"Always. Why don't you go choose one?"

She rushed over to the bookcase in the corner of the room. The bookcase was also disorganised and messy and chaotic, much like the dishevelled mess of toys, and Lily's small bedroom, and the single bathroom shared between three users. Compared to his life, hers was a disaster, yet she still seemed happy—something a stroppy rich man such as Brian found difficult to comprehend.

"How about this one?" Lily asked, returning to Brian's side with a large book about a talking tractor.

"Looks perfect."

Lily was the one thing that had come out of his sister's marriage that Brian appreciated. He adored her. He lived for his ill-timed and unannounced visits to the house when he could read with her, or play with her, or go for a walk with her. He occasionally featured her in his videos—something Mike protested about with a vehemence that Brian ignored —and his followers always liked and shared those videos the most.

She was the only thing Brian seemed to care about more than himself.

"We're having Christmas as a family this year," Clarissa announced, still in the doorway.

"That's fine," Brian said, opening the book. "What time's lunch?"

"No, Brian, I mean as a family—just this family."

"Huh?"

"As in, with just Mike and our daughter."

"Oh. What am I supposed to do?" Before she could answer, he interrupted and said, "Fine. Don't care. Don't want another year of tasting Mike's shit attempts at cooking anyway."

"Please don't swear in front of Lily."

"Shove it up your arse." He started reading with an animated, excited voice, "Timmy the Tractor was sitting outside the farmer's house."

It was difficult for any observer to deduce whether Brian's sister not including him in their Christmas Day plans had bothered him. He moved over it so quickly, so desperate to appear impervious to it, that he gave little time to acknowledging it.

At least, that's how it appeared.

In truth, as he read the menial children's story, he paid little attention to the words he was speaking; his mind was elsewhere, considering what he was going to do on the 25th of December now—he hardly had anyone else to spend it with, did he? Their parents had passed away five years ago. Brain had spent their entire funeral trying to appear as unaffected as possible, but the façade became tougher at Christmas—he missed his mother's Christmas dinner and the games his dad organised, even if he'd given the impression that he hated it all.

Perhaps he could call one of the women he'd shagged and see if they wished to spend the day with him; then again, he'd hardly given them a reason to bestow such charity on him.

In the end he figured, fuck it, it was only Christmas. Not like it meant much. It was a load of shit. Just another way to ensure that capitalism thrived. Jesus wasn't real, and if he was, he sounded like a dick, and Brian didn't particularly wish to celebrate his birth. What was a day on his own, anyway? He spent every other day alone, it was just one more.

The news, however, gave him the urge to leave; he did not want Mike to see any weakness in his frown—he would not give him the satisfaction. So, once he had rushed through the story, he denied Lily's request to read another, and gave Lily the biggest hug he could, knowing that, for the first Christmas Day in her life, he would not be there. And he left. Ignoring Mike's folded arms in the kitchen, and ignoring Clarissa's bowed head—they'd evidently just had a conversation where Clarissa had argued the case for having her brother there, even if just for lunch. Mike, however, remained stern and adamant. And, just as had been the case ever since he'd entered their lives, Mike's opinion countered Brian's. The man who had been there for seven years would have more influence over his sister's decisions than the brother who'd been there since the day she was born.

As he stepped onto the driveway and avoided slipping on the ice, he felt his sister's presence in the doorway behind him.

"Hey, Brian."

"What?"

"Happy Christmas."

He stared at her. Saw the conflict in her face. Noticed Lily standing behind her. Heard a clattering of Mike making tea with an anger no doubt caused by Brian's presence.

"You too," he said, smiled at Lily, then turned away and plodded down the street.

He approached his Ferrari, intentionally parked in the most prominent place of the street so everyone would know he was better than them, and paused as he opened the door. He bowed his head, just slightly. As he fought away tears, he caught sight of something from the corner of his eye.

By the time he'd turned his head fully, I was gone, and Brian wasn't sure what he'd seen.

But the thought was still there.

The uneasy feeling. The doubt. The turbulence in his logical reasoning.

He shook it off, climbed into his Ferrari, and drove home, unaware that, this time tomorrow, he was going to have the most eventful night of his life.

CHAPTER
SIX

Brian woke on Christmas Eve the same way he awoke most days—during the afternoon and with an incessant hangover.

He stepped out of bed, trudged down the stairs, put the coffee machine on, and leant topless against the kitchen counter. He cranked up the thermostat and, as he rubbed his temples, the luxury of having a warm home went unnoticed. He didn't waste a moment considering the financial or environmental implications of filling so many unused rooms with heat—he had come to expect such standards.

He spent a bit of time on the sofa, watching whatever tacky Christmas film was on Sky, staring numbly at his 85-inch plasma Ultra HD television as he swallowed a spoonful of milk and sugary hoops. It didn't take long for him to get bored—about eight minutes to be exact—and he picked up his phone to check the comments on his latest video. They were mostly positive and provided him with many unearned hits of dopamine.

. . .

Totally awesome dude

U r the fucking shit m8

Check out my naked videos at TripleXXXSandy

That last one was spam, and he marked it as such.

Still, despite the welcome reception for what was essentially a video of him frying bacon (yes, that's as basic as his profile was), he felt something he refused to acknowledge.

Most would call it loneliness.

He dismissed it as a feeling he didn't feel. How could he be lonely when he was so loved by so many people?

Still, it would be nice to have some company on Christmas Eve. And on Christmas Day, seeing as he would spend that alone too.

He opened his phone book and scrolled through the names he had contacted most recently. Most were women whose names he did not remember, and had provided nicknames instead: *weird boobs; ginger girl; loud bitch from ritz; annoying but hot; always talking vegan.* You get the gist...

Then he came upon a woman with a name.

Tiffany.

She had been nice. A little too made up, yes, but she had actually spoken to him. Gotten to know him. Asked him questions. Most of these women just smiled and nodded, but she had seemed genuinely interested in him, and he wondered if she would be up for seeing him again this evening.

With a confidence he did not deserve, he pressed her

name and put the phone to his ear. Eventually, she answered.

"Hello?"

"Tiffany?"

"Yes?"

"It's Brian."

"Brian?"

"We met the other... I, I'm the guy with the videos."

"Oh, yeah. Brian. What's up?"

"Well, not much, I... I was just wondering if you wanted to meet up?"

"Meet up?"

"Yeah. Like tonight."

There was a moment of silence.

"You're kidding, right?"

"No, I'm not up to much, and I thought we had fun—"

"Fun?"

"Yeah."

"Oh sure, we had a load of fun—a whole fifteen seconds of it."

"Yeah, look, I mean... I don't know. I thought you might want to meet up again or something."

"It's Christmas Eve."

"I know."

"And you fucked me three weeks ago, and this is the first time you've spoken to me since."

"Yeah..."

"Listen, Brian, do you have anyone there with you? Or are you just bored and lonely and don't want to be reduced to wanking on Christmas?"

"Look, if you don't–"

"Tell you what, Brain, if you ever do like someone—like, actually like them—don't fuck them like a charging bull and sulk when they don't say it was amazing after you cum before they even know you've started. And especially then don't ignore them for three weeks, then phone me them up on Christmas Eve because you're lonely and have got no one else to talk to."

"Oh, fuck you."

"Fuck me?"

"Yes. You were shit. And your tits look fake."

"Hah! This is brilliant..."

"You know what? I don't even want to see you."

"Then why are we having this conversation?"

"I—I don't know."

"Have a lovely Christmas, Brian."

"Fuck you, bitch."

She laughed. Genuine laughter. Overzealous laughter. At him. How dare she.

He went to aim another insult at her, but hung up instead. He convinced himself he was worth more than her, and that she was a shit lay, and what does he need a skank like that for, anyway?

He scrolled through his phone book for another woman, but the prospect of a similar exchange made calling any of them too daunting. Instead, he marched to the bedroom, opened his laptop, went to Porn Hub (the browser suggested it as soon as he typed P), searched *Milf Anal Gang Bang* and clicked on the first video he saw.

He came almost straight away.

The pleasure didn't last long. A few seconds, maybe. It wasn't that great. He didn't even move afterwards. He just sat there. Alone. With a sticky belly and an empty house.

The video continued playing. Some older women with massive tits begged a guy with an unrealistically big penis (like, seriously) to fuck her in the arse. It only made Brian feel more ashamed, and as he looked down at the mess, up at the screen, down at the mess, and up at the screen, he wondered, not for the first time, what was wrong with him.

He sighed. Wiped his hands on a dirty t-shirt that he'd left draped over the back of his chair. Then he pushed himself to his feet and traipsed through the corridor toward the bathroom. As he did, he caught sight of himself in the mirror that hung on the wall, and he paused. Noticed the bags under his eyes. The mess of his hair. The semen dripping down his snail trail.

He truly hated the person who looked back at him.

Not just disliked him—he *hated* him. Vehemently. With a passion and a rage he found hard to quell.

He punched the mirror, smashing it into several pieces, and felt better for a moment. A brief moment, as he looked down at his hand to find there was now blood on his knuckles.

"Fucking dick."

He went into the bathroom as if nothing had happened, took clumps of toilet paper in his fist, and wiped away the mess before dumping it into the already open toilet.

He didn't even notice me sitting on the edge of the bath.

CHAPTER

SEVEN

"Good afternoon, Brian."

"Holy fuck!" He fell back, grabbed the shower curtain to keep himself steady, failed, collapsed on the floor, then quickly stood to face me. "Who the fuck are you?"

"You know who I am."

"What the fuck!"

His lexical choices left something to be desired—but I am used to such shock. People are rarely expecting to see me, regardless of how much effect I have on their everyday lives.

I usually just wait for it to pass.

Denial is the most common and equally the most tedious part of the process—for Brian, however, it was highly amusing. He looked like an animal who was about to become roadkill, barely able to decide which way to look. His eyes darted to the mirror, to the sink, to me, to the door —which he considered running for, but didn't as he'd have to cross my path—then pinched himself and looked back at me. It was the noises he made that most tickled me—*uh,*

39

bah, meh, wha, hoo, puh, naaaa, waaa, oh, shiii, fuuu, hollobollo. At one point, I swear he even went cross-eyed.

"Are you quite done yet?" I asked, unable to hide my smirk. I sat back, my manner casual, my tail relaxed, being as patient as I could be with this piece of shit.

"No, you're—you're not fucking real—you're not..."

"If I wasn't real, could I do this?" Brian grabbed his arse as the momentary sensation of a giant ladle being rammed up his anus made his body spasm.

He backed up against the wall, as if those extra few inches away from me would make any difference when I could torment him without even raising my claw.

"Oh, Brian, don't be so tedious, we both know why I'm here."

"No—it—it can't be, I thought I'd made it up, imagined it, I was close to death, I—I thought it wasn't real..."

"Well, my little vagabond, do I look unreal?"

He surveyed me, mouth hanging open, looking from my feet to my horns, eyes wide, finally taking me in.

I suppose my devilish appearance—excuse the pun—is quite something to comprehend for a human. I dress well, wearing a suit to make my initial appearance a little less intimidating (it helps them pass through the denial stage quicker), but I can still do nothing to hide my blood red skin, or my slashing, pointed tail, or my large, curved horns.

"Fuck..."

"Yes, fuck indeed. Now, can we get on with this? I have a four o'clock I wish to attend to. We always butt fuck Jeffrey Dahmer on Christmas Eve, and I'd hate to miss it."

"You... you do what?"

I stand. His body trembles and he flattens himself against the far wall. How ridiculous.

"You remember the deal, don't you?"

"Deal?"

I put the palm of my claw against his head, and he tried to flee before realising he cannot flee a room when I am blocking the exit. Within a few seconds, I'd replayed our first meeting in his mind, saving me the monotony of recounting it for him verbally.

"Debt..." he said. "What debt? What was the debt?"

"I saved your life, Brian. You were braindead, and I gave you breath. Are you not grateful?"

"Yes... very grateful... So very grateful..."

"And I gave you seven years of good luck—good luck that you have thoroughly enjoyed, have you not?"

"Luck?"

"Yes, luck. Do you really think so many people would willingly watch such monotonous, inept videos without a great deal of luck? This house, the women, everything you have—it is due to luck."

"Yes, I am grateful, I really am."

"Grateful does nothing. I am here to collect my debt. One for every year."

"What—what do I owe you?" He looked around, as if he was going to find something I wanted in his bathroom. "I— I have money. Lots of it. How much do you want?"

I laughed—a laugh that boomed throughout the house and vibrated his bones. I intensified the fire in my eyes and increased the shadows of the room, and he shat himself like a little girl—no, scrap that, it is offensive to little girls—he shat himself like a pathetic simpleton who had earned nothing he had.

"I gave you your money, you insolent nuisance! You think I want it back?"

"Hits, then? Yes, I could recommend your videos, and then you could get lots of views, and I–"

"Silence!"

He made himself smaller, as small as he could, shrinking into a ball in the corner of the room, cowering, quivering, looking up at me with his entire body trembling.

"I want a life."

"A life?"

"Yes. One for each year of good luck."

"Seven lives?"

"You can count, can you not?"

"Yes, but I don't know what you mean..."

Don't know what I mean?

Was this boy as thick as he was pitiful?

"You will kill a human for each year I have given you—that is your debt."

"What? I can't kill anyone."

"You will. And you have until noon tomorrow to repay your debt."

"But I—"

"I will deliver a name to you. And a location. And an image, if need be. You will end that person's life, or face the consequences." I smiled, bent down, and patted him on the head. "There's a good boy."

Satisfied that he had received my message, I turned to go. And that was when I heard it—so small I might not have heard it if it weren't for me being all powerful and omnipotent, and so little that I could barely fathom that he had the audacity.

"No."

I paused.

Turned.

Glared at him.

"No?" I repeated.

"No. I won't do it. Y—y—you can't make me."

"Can't I?"

He tried to scamper away, tried to crawl past me, tried to outwit a creature the supremacy of which he could not even begin to fathom.

I raised my arms and, in an instant, everything he knew flew above him—his ceilings, his floor, his sky, his dirt, his earth—and he fell upon a large slab of cracked stone beside my ankles. The pits of Hell raged around me, lava spewing over mounds of stone, fire reaching for the scorched orange sky, and screams across the distance creating the beautiful harmony that accompanied the sinister scenes.

"See this?" I said, looking down upon him, enjoying my performance as he lay on his back, shivering, crying, shuddering. I could smell the shit that stained his pants, such was the depths of his fear.

"I said *see this*?"

He nodded, sweat dripping down his face, mixing with his tears.

"This is only the beginning of your eternal damnation should you fail me!"

He backed away, trying to crawl, but with a raise of my claw I summoned him into the air, and he hung in front of me like a feather on the wind.

"Your followers, your money, your life—all of it will go, and you will experience the death you deserved when that bus smashed your skull into your brain."

I lifted my other claw and fire rose around us, surrounding his body, gripping his legs, burning his skin, and for a minute—one whole joyous minute—I let him feel what it was like to be burned to death, but to never actually die.

Then I dropped my claws and allowed him to thud on the ground.

"Feel that?" I said. "That will be forever."

He wept, unable to look up at me, sobbing, a wreck of a man—he was something lower than human, something even more despicable than he was when I brought him here.

I let him feel the aftereffects of the agony and, as I did, my eyes wandered over the surroundings. In the distance, I noticed a demon buttfucking Jeffrey Dahmer. Damn, I missed it.

"Do you understand me?" I asked.

He nodded with such weakness I could taste it.

"Then hurry—you don't have long."

I raised my arms and the surroundings disappeared, and he found himself on his sofa, in his house, his body restored, but still not forgetting what had happened to him.

The television was on, but no Christmas movie was playing. There was simply an image, a location, and a name.

Brian, despite whatever little intelligence I have seen in him, understood what it meant.

And as he stared at the name—Gus Phillips—he recalled hearing that name on the news. (Not that he often watched the news, but occasionally videos came up on TikTok that informed him of current events—ones that he quickly skipped so he could get to the videos of women dancing in skimpy outfits.) And, as he recalled this man, he realised that his first target completely deserved the death Brian was fated to bestow upon him.

DEBT #1 GUS PHILLIPS

EIGHT

Gus Phillips was a cunt.

There is no other way to put it.

I know you probably get offended by the word—honestly, I feel the same about the word *moist*; it sends shivers down my body, which may be surprising considering I have dedicated my unlife to torturing those unfortunate enough to have deserved it, but I still can't help finding the word revolting—nevertheless, I can find no better word to describe this man, and once I explain to you who this cretin is, I think that, whatever reaction you have to the word, you will undoubtedly agree it is the most apt.

Especially considering Gus Phillips was a child rapist and a wife killer.

He had molested his daughter, and his daughter's friend, and murdered his wife after she'd found out about it. The murder case went to trial, but without his wife's body to give the prosecution vital evidence (he'd put in an incinerator a week before anyone knew she was missing), he was found not guilty. There was an image on the news of him in court after the verdict was read out, turning over his shoulder and grinning at his daughter (who had since become an adult, and therefore no longer provoked any sexual interest from him.) He has offended many times since then, having learned the best ways to evade the police's threshold for evidence that is required to see a case go to trial.

And before anyone suggests he didn't do it—he did.

I know this shit, I am The Devil; he fucking did it.

And everyone else knew he was guilty too. And he knew everyone else knew he was guilty. But he didn't give a shit—he sat in his caravan with his stained vests and his potbelly and his receding hairline and his glum smirk and his gingivitis between the few teeth he had left and his wrinkled skin that appeared misplaced on a 43-year-old and his cock covered in flakes of smegma, knowing there was nothing anyone could do to stop him. His IQ when it came to empathy or intellectuality or conversational ability was immensely low—but his IQ when it came to knowing how to avoid the threshold of evidence required by CPS was genius. He was a sex offender unlike any other sex offender —he had gone without being caught for so long that he'd become an expert at getting away with it.

Yes, many honourable vigilantes had sought their own violent justice against him, but they'd never achieved it.

Why?

Because, when such events occur, Gus had the audacity to call the police on his attackers. And the police would show up, arrest his attackers, and those attackers would be charged. And he'd laugh. And some cheap, tacky newspaper would sensationalise the story to sell their agenda against the establishment, spreading news of how society lets the honourable suffer while the abhorrent prosper. And that, my friend, is the sorry state your little world is in.

So, going back to my original assertion with this man, whatever you think of the word, I have no doubt you now agree:

He was a cunt.

A complete and utter cunt.

And, on this particular Christmas Eve, when Brian had been given the instruction to bring demise to this repugnant ingrate, Gus was in his caravan, watching reruns of some dodgy adult cartoon that towed the line between being funny and being offensive, whilst a girl in her early teens laid on his floor, so fucked up on repeated injections of Rohypnol that she had no idea what was going on.

Brian, as despicable as he may be, was nothing compared to this lowlife. In fact, once Brian learned of this man's past, he came to terms with killing him pretty quickly. After all, he would be doing the world a service, and most of us would thank him for it. Of course, Brian was not at all acquitted with the ability to dispose of a revolting oaf such as this creature—in fact, Brian had never so much as been in a fight in his entire life—but I will get to Brian shortly. First, let's return to the cunt and get to know him a little better as we eagerly anticipate his destruction.

As I was saying, on this Christmas Eve, he was sitting on the cheap cushions of what was his sofa, but when rearranged later, would become his bed. He gazed between the brown sickly curtains of his stained caravan window, ogling a group of young girls walking by. He grinned and leered at them, resenting how winter made them cover up, reminiscing about the short skirts of the summer.

They noticed him and grimaced.

He didn't care.

He stared, persistent and unrelenting, and they quickened their pace. With a sneer and a chuckle, he returned to his cartoon.

The girl made a noise. A little drool fell from her mouth. She wore his daughter's old school uniform, and she rolled over a little, her greasy blond hair falling over her face. She groaned, coming around slightly. Not much—you couldn't talk to her, and nor could she talk to you—but enough for her eyes to flicker open and for her to look at the disgusting ogre sitting over her.

"Happy Christmas," he said in a thick west country accent.

Now she was awake, he would help himself to a little Christmas present.

He held her up by the hair, shoved her torso against the edge of the cushions with her droopy eyes pressed against the cold glass, pulled her hips into the air, and lifted the skirt away from her naked arse. Her body was floppy and needed propping up. He gripped her skin to keep her in place, and thrusted hard.

When he was done, he dumped her on the floor and shoved a pasty that was three days past its expiration date in the microwave. As it cooked, he took an open jar of baby food from the cupboard and sniffed it. It made even Gus flinch, such was the stench, and that is saying something— the odour that protruded from him and his caravan was vile, and for an odour to stick out from the general stink of his caravan meant that the odour must be sickening.

Nevertheless, he took a teaspoon, lifted the girl's head up by her hair, and shoved spoonful after spoonful between her dainty cracked lips.

She didn't swallow, not at first, and he had to force it down her throat with his chubby fingers. Eventually, she came around enough to swallow, and he poured the rest of the mould-encrusted food down her mouth.

Once done, he dumped her on the floor next to a dog bowl of water and devoured his pasty. She didn't drink any, but it was there if she needed it. He didn't want her to die, after all—he was not interested in fucking a corpse.

An older lady walked by. One who'd moaned at his being here; who'd asked the police to get rid of him, only to be told there was nothing they could do; who'd looked for ways to buy a caravan on another site so she didn't have to pass him, only to realise that a lifetime on the dole left her with little in the way of pension to acquire a new living space. He stuck his thumb up at her through a gap in the curtains as she passed. The lady looked away, shook her head, and hurried onwards.

With his afternoon's excursions finished, he sat back and watched more television, unbothered by the food smeared across his cheeks and the stickiness on his fingers. After half an hour or so, his eyes drooped, and his head lolled, and with no job or family or friends to visit, and with his guest quite unconscious, he gave himself permission to nap, which ended up becoming a heavy slumber.

He slept, and he snored, and he dreamed—providing a perfect opportunity for a certain man to take Gus's wretched life from him.

NINE

How does one kill a man?

It was not a question Brian had ever considered before. Not seriously, anyway. Of course, he'd speculated. He'd considered whether he could dig the knife he used to slice apart his apple tart into his brother-in-law's throat before the sisterfucker fought him off, and he occasionally wondered how he might dispose of someone hogging the middle lane of the motorway and whether, if he knocked his car into their car, he would survive with both his life and no prison sentence. Nevertheless, these were not abnormal thoughts, and they were usually fleeting.

(Oh, and by the way, in case you might object to the enlightening fact that murderous thoughts are not abnormal, and are about to declare that you've never had one – don't bother. I'm The Devil. I've seen inside your head. I know what thoughts you conceal, even from yourself, and you are secretly a murderous fucker just like everyone.)

Now, however, if Brian was to give the logistics of murder serious thought, he had to actually come to terms with the fact that he was going to murder someone. He did not have too many grievances about taking the life of such a man as Gus Phillips—I don't imagine many of us would—but he was concerned about what might happen should he fail.

This man had killed before, and his own wife, no less. What might Gus do to a stranger who had the audacity to attempt to take his life?

Brian needed a plan.

No, he needed a gun.

But this was the UK, and you could hardly just walk into a gun store and buy one. He was sure that you could acquire one should you know the right people, but Brian didn't. He barely knew any people, but those few he did were not particularly gangsta. Most of his social interactions were with other online gamers on Call of Duty, and the closest they came to being mean was threatening to fuck a stranger's mum when they blew up their avatar.

No, a gun was not a potential.

A sharp knife, then?

He had plenty. Not that he ever used them—he mostly ordered takeout, or ate out, or bought a chef for an evening. He wasn't actually sure where things were in his kitchen. And he could hardly just use an ordinary cutlery knife, he'd need a big knife, like a butcher's knife, one that he'd seen his guest chefs use to slice meat.

He searched his kitchen draws and found such a knife. He tucked it down the back of his belt as if he was sheathing a sword, but the feel of the steel against his buttocks brought the stark reality of the situation crashing down upon him, and he felt that a knife wasn't a good idea.

But what else was there?

Poison, perhaps?

He could pour some bleach down the guy's throat, or put it in his evening brew.

But did he even have any bleach?

He employed cleaners, and most of them brought their own stuff. He wasn't sure he'd even know where to get some.

Weed-killer then?

But again, that was his gardener's domain!

He thought through every room in his house, trying to imagine what was in there, and what he could use.

Bathroom: shampoo, soap, dead flowers on the windowsill, rubber duck, toothpaste, toothbrush, toilet roll, grubby towel, grubby bath mat.

Bedroom: hand lotion, tissue paper, fresh toilet roll, crusted toilet roll, pillows, clock, phone charger, women's underwear (don't ask.)

Living room: television, sofa, cushions, footrest, coffee table, curtains.

No, there was nothing else. Unless he was going to hit the guy with a rubber duck, shock him with a grubby bath mat, then threaten to charge his phone, there was nothing else to use but the knife.

But there was one thing! He thought of it as he made his way to the door. Some woman had bought those fluffy handcuffs around that one time, and she'd left them. But where did she leave them?

He searched his bedroom and found them in his bedside draw. Pink and fluffy. Not sure why the fluff was there, they still hurt to wear. It must be purely for decoration. Still, it had been a fun night.

He shoved them into his back pocket, checked the knife was still in his belt, and made for the front door, ready to do this, full of adrenaline and full of vigour, supplied with a location from myself, and with enough stupidity to try to pull it off and–

And the doorbell rang.

Just as he went to open the door, the doorbell rang.

He hesitated, worried it would be me again. But it wasn't. He opened the door, allowing his sister to barge in before he could object.

"Brian, I have had enough. It's time we talk about this."

When they were children, his mother would sometimes nag his father, then his father would turn to Brian, raise his eyebrows, say she was "on one", then do whatever she instructed him to do.

Well, it seemed like Clarissa was "on one" now. Her hair was a wet mess, suggesting it had been raining outside; her arms were moving quickly, going between being folded and wildly gesticulating; and her voice was all over the place, chaotic and uneven.

"Hey, Clarissa, now's not really a good time," he said, albeit weakly—he wasn't particularly a man of gumption.

"Good time? When is it ever a good time with you? When you're off making your videos? When you're sitting around your fancy house with your feet up watching porn in ultra-HD?"

"Look—"

"How much do you even earn to maintain this house?"

"I–"

"A plastic toy truck, Brian! Do you know what I'm talking about? A plastic toy truck—that is what you got your niece for Christmas last year. A fiver from some shitty toy store you stopped at on the way so you didn't feel guilty. You make all this money, and you gave her a truck. And, in case you didn't realise, she is a *girl*!"

"Girls can like trucks..."

"It's not even about the truck, Brian! It's about Mike. And why you must always be a dick. I love having you around because Lily loves having you around. She adores you. You're her fun uncle and not the fuckup we all think you are."

Brian looked around his big house. "I don't think I'm a fuckup..."

"That's just it, Brian! You don't think anything unless it's about you. I wanted you there at Christmas, but Mike couldn't stand it, and if you had just, for one minute, pulled your head out of your arse and tried to be nice to him, maybe we'd get to pretend that we are a family!"

Brian looked at his watch. He noticed her eyes widening at the audacity of his impatience, but he couldn't hang around—he had until sometime tomorrow (midday, was it?) and seven people to kill (fuck, seven?). As much as he was willing to stand there and be shouted at, he just couldn't do it right now.

"Look, I really have to be somewhere–"

"No! Whatever it is, whatever her name is, you cancel it, or her, or whatever—and we can actually talk, and you can pretend to be a caring big brother." She shook her head and placed her hands on her hips. "Big brother... You're supposed to take care of me, but who spent their adolescence pulling whose head out of the toilet when they'd come home pissed, huh?"

Brian looked at the door.

"Don't even think about going!"

"Look, I really can't do this right now. I'm happy to talk, but right now, I just, I have to go."

He turned. Placed his hand on the door handle. Opened the door.

"If you leave now, you'll never see Lily."

He paused. Stood in the open doorway. Unable to go, but knowing he desperately needed to.

"You can't do that," he said, his voice small compared to hers.

"Oh, can't I?"

"That's cruel to Lily."

"Is it? At least she'd be left with nice memories of seeing you through a child's eyes, and would not have to grow up and be disappointed with who you really are."

Now that hurt.

"Look..." She saw that she'd taken it too far, and she placed her hands on his arms. "What's more important to you than me? We're family. Lily adores you. I adore you. Sometimes, not so much, but most of the time, yeah, you're okay, and I enjoy having you around in those rare moments when you're not being vain or being a dick. I just want... I want you to seem like you're actually happy."

He laughed. He didn't expect to, he didn't even decide to, but somehow, it came out. "Happy?"

"Yes."

"I don't even know what that word means."

He pulled away from her grip and continued down the driveway.

"We'll talk," he shouted back as he opened the door to his Mercedes and climbed in. "Do not take Lily away from me. We will talk. I... I'll do better... I..."

Fearing that he might make a promise he couldn't keep, he shut the door, turned the ignition, put the heater on full blast and the music up loud, and pulled away.

He couldn't bring himself to look at her in the rear-view mirror.

Once he had turned the corner, he pulled the car over and put the caravan park into his GPS. It wasn't far. The knife pressed against his waist. The handcuffs dug into his arse.

He pulled onto the road and drove fast, thoughts of his niece stopping him from focusing.

By the time he'd pulled up at the caravan park, it was dark—as late afternoon is in December—and he was focused, and he was ready.

Oh, and he was shitting himself.

TEN

When Brian was at school, his peers had thrown around insults such as *gyppo* and *pikey* like they were giving out sweets.

But not Brian.

Brian did his best not to judge.

Which was unusual, as he was an incredibly judgemental person, keen to sneer at anyone he deemed to have faults—whether it was parents with loud children, vapid woman who dated misogynistic blokes for their six-pack, or teenagers who called their friends *mush,* he did not hide his disdain—but when it came to people who would probably kick his arse, he tended to be remarkably unopinionated.

Just like in this field full of caravans.

Here, he made sure his face remained neutral.

All because of an incident he'd witnessed when he was at school, when a girl with frilly hair and a face of acne once called someone a *gyppo/pikey*. She had been knocked to the floor with a single punch, dragged out of school by her hair, and kicked in the head until a teacher intervened.

He'd never seen this girl at school again.

Ever since then, Brian had been full of respect for the traveller community, and disapproved of all derogatory terms one might use against them.

Even so, he left his Mercedes around the corner from the caravan park, as it boasted a shiny silver body, and he didn't want anyone to steal it. This did mean, however, that he had to walk to Row 4 Caravan B.

And Brian was aware of every set of eyes that turned toward him and recognised him as a stranger—especially the teenagers who hung around in large groups wearing tacky tracksuits and eat-shit-and-die facial expressions that Brian found quite intimidating. He put his hood up, his hands in his pockets, and avoided making eye contact with anyone in hopes of avoiding trouble. He had always taken pleasure in intimidating strangers with his dark clothing and angry expression, believing such an image made him appear menacing—but he was still a middle-class white kid with a decent education and a privilege he wasn't aware of. The people in these caravans were the actual intimidating people—these were the people others went out of their way to avoid upsetting, and as much as he refused to admit he felt unsafe, he was terrified.

A man approached, and ceased his stride with an abruption that made Brain shake, and stared at him as he passed. Brian kept his head down. In a community where everyone knew everyone, a stranger was easily recognisable. He kept his fist wrapped around the knife in his pocket, not that he wished to use it; if he hurt one of them, he'd be outnumbered in an instant.

But what about Gus Phillips?

Would they try to defend him?

Or would they feel differently about a rapist?

As he approached Row 4 Caravan B, he noticed it was

the only one with no Christmas lights. The area surrounding it seemed cold and deserted, with the weeds and grass overgrown and neglected. There were so many shadows crawling across its exterior, it was as if the moon had ignored this one caravan. The words *fuck off yuh scum* were graffitied diagonally across the door, obscured by dirt, suggesting they had been there for a while. Perhaps Gus had grown tired of removing the graffiti, so he just let this one stay there.

Gus, it appeared, was not wanted here.

Brian wondered if these people would be grateful to anyone who would remove this stain from their community. However differently they lived, and however alien their culture was to Brian, they would concur that Gus was a maggot—something unwanted, like an infestation of cockroaches—and no one would bemoan someone exterminating this vermin.

The next obstacle was the murder itself.

Inside the caravan was dark, suggesting Gus was asleep. Or that he was hanging around in the dark. Or that he was watching television. Who knew?

Brian looked to his left, then his right. He was alone. No kids wandered around here. No strangers stared at intruders. It was neglected and unvisited. Unwanted and solitary. Decrepit and alone.

This, at least, would work in Brian's favour.

He approached the caravan, took out his knife, and paused by the door.

He went to place his hand on the door handle, then thought—*what the fuck am I doing?*

Was he really just going to burst in and stab the guy?

What if the guy resisted? Took Brian's knife off him?

Gutted him? Killed him and sent him to Hell—the precise place he was trying to avoid?

More pertinently—what if Brian was hit by his conscience at the last moment? What if doubt set in? What if he swung his knife, only to find his arm stiffen and stop the impact, such is the self-restraint his ethics might bring about within him?

He took a deep breath. Reminded himself who this guy was. Rapist. Murderer. Scum of the Earth. This guy deserved to die. Brian was helping the world. It would have been the right thing to do, even if he hadn't been tasked with doing it.

He made the decision that he would do it. That he would not let his conscience hold him back. That he was going to kill this guy, and he wouldn't hesitate.

He just had to burst in, surprise Gus, and aim for the throat.

Deep breath.

This was only the first of seven. He didn't have time to contemplate it.

And with that, he pressed down on the door handle, burst the door open, and jumped on a figure that laid in the darkness on the floor. He held the knife high above his head, brought it down, and stopped.

This was a woman.

"Huh?"

She was vaguely conscious, moving her head to the side, groaning, opening and shutting her eyes. Distant. Unaware. She was naked, too. This wasn't who Brian was after.

He stood. Looked around.

There were plates with pizza crusts on the sofa. Babestation on television. Dirty socks on the floor. The place was even more disgusting inside than it was out. But there was no Gus Phillips. Just a woman, evidently used and soon to be discarded.

"Where..."

He searched every corner, but there weren't many corners to search.

Evidently, Gus Phillips wasn't here.

Which was odd, as this was where I'd sent him. Why would I send him there if Gus Phillips wasn't there?

He put his knife in his pocket. His hands on his hips. Shook his head. Assumed I had given him the wrong information.

But I am never, ever wrong.

Never.

And at that very moment the toilet flushed, Gus Phillips emerged from a door, and he cast his eyes over the coward standing beside his holiday treat.

ELEVEN

"What the fucking fuck?" Gus demanded.

He charged toward Brian, his chubby fingers reaching for his intruder, and Brain did not fumble for his knife quickly enough. Gus's fat hands wrapped around Brian's throat as he took his opponent to the ground and mounted him, squeezing hard on his oesophagus.

"This is my home—I can kill you legally!"

Brian coughed and spluttered and choked, struggling for air, desperate for oxygen. He reached his hands up, pushed at Gus's face, but the bastard was too heavy. He could not breathe, but could still smell the rancid odour of Gus's breath, the body odour from his pits, and the cheesy shit smell of his vest.

It surprised Brian how quickly he accepted death; how soon he thought, *ah, well, this is how I go.*

His eyes set on the woman across the floor from him. Her eyelids lifted hazily, they made eye contact, and they were momentarily united in a moment of reciprocal suffering. They were both hurt by the same perpetrator. In a way,

Brian was the fortunate one—Gus was willing to grant him the sweet release of death.

Death.

It was coming soon.

And Hell was waiting.

No, Brian decided. He would not end up wrecked like her. He would not let this fucker destroy him. He would not be another story for the newspapers to tell; another sting of guilt for his sister; another victim of another scumbag.

This fucker was going down.

A head rush overcame him. Blots filled his vision. Death was imminent, and he felt distant from his body. Despite this, he still found the strength to reach his right hand toward his pocket, wrap his fingers around his knife, draw it out, and hold it high above them, behind Gus's head so he could not see. Brian's eyes widened and, with the last bit of energy left in his muscles, he brought the knife down upon the flab of Gus's back, barely penetrating but penetrating enough to cause the arsehole to cry out in pain and loosen his grip on Brian's throat.

Brian sucked in air, but he didn't waste any time relishing it—he stabbed the fucker in his side, forced him onto his back, and stabbed him again. And again. And again. And again, and again, and again.

Gus tried to reach for the knife, but the pain was too much, and his attempts were feeble. Brian shoved the knife in his belly, and it almost became stuck in the folds, and he had to twist it to release it from the flesh—Brian didn't have that much strength, and it was difficult to penetrate Gus's fatty insulation—but he managed, and he kept stabbing and stabbing and stabbing.

Gus lifted his head up, let out a roaring bellow, and in doing so, exposed his throat. Brian swung at Gus's neck with all the strength he could conjure, and he was pleasantly surprised to find himself able to shove the knife into the sicko's windpipe.

Gus grabbed his neck, blood cascading between the cracks of his fingers, and thrashed around the floor with a franticity only found in the most desperate of fools, slamming feet against draws and cupboards, knocking the television over; as if throwing himself around in a manic state would do anything to defer death.

Brian stood, knife by his side, his face covered in a spray of Gus's blood. Gus backed away and shoved himself against the door, which duly opened; he fell out of the caravan and onto the wet grass outside.

Brian remained still for a moment, relishing intakes of oxygen. He could hear Gus spluttering and struggling outside, and even though he had no frame of reference, he was sure these were the sounds of death.

A desire to get the hell out of there overcame him.

He charged to the door, then stopped. Turned his head. Looked back at the woman, laid on the floor, hair clumped into balls of grease, dirty and used, barely awake.

He couldn't leave her here. What if she died? What if help didn't come in time?

Knowing this was not part of the plan but unable to do anything else, he scooped his arms beneath her neck and her legs and hoisted her up. He almost dropped her, struggling under the weight, despite her being a petite woman. (Brian was not a physically fit man.) Still, he persevered, and held her tight as he carried her outside.

Gus tried one last time to push himself to his knees, but he was too weak. He slumped onto his front as his final breath left his body. There was a potent smell of faeces, and Brian wondered if Gus had shat himself before he died.

Brian hesitated, noticing the crowd that had gathered. Dozens of them. Standing around the caravan, staring at Brian, in their tracksuits and vests, with their beer and cider, and with their angry faces. They looked at the body, then at Brian, then at the body, then at Brian. Aware of how much the travelling community protected their own, Brian panicked, terrified they would take revenge. Loyalty was everything to these people.

But they didn't attack him.

In fact, quite the contrary—something strange and beautifully bizarre happened.

They applauded.

It happened suddenly. One person started, then everyone joined in, a crowd of strangers smacking their hands together with vehemence and pride. They beamed at Brian, big smiles in his direction, and the applause grew grander and keener.

He walked between them, his arms shaking as he carried the woman, and they thanked him as he left. Words of gratitude guided him out, appreciations such as "You wonderful man" and "Thank you for getting rid of him" accompanying smiles of relief and promises of secrecy. They would answer the police's questions of what the man who took this cretin's life looked like, but every answer would be incorrect and inconsistent. Some would say he was an old ginger fellow, others would say he was a crazed infant, some might even say he was an obese woman. Anything but the truth would be provided to the detectives who investigated this man's demise.

Whatever happened, no witness testimony would confirm or condemn Brain for what they perceived to be an act of favour, rather than malice.

He reached his car and, despite the mess she would

make on his back seat, placed the woman on it. He drove under the speed limit so as not to attract attention, and down country roads where CCTV would not pick him up. He pulled into the bay of the A&E section of the nearest hospital, put his hood up, opened the back door, dragged the woman out, and left her on the pavement.

Without another glance back, he returned to his car and drove away.

CHAPTER

TWELVE

B rian didn't stop driving. He considered whether to return home, but he didn't want to return to a place that made him think of life as easy—he still had too much to do—so he remained on the dual carriageway, circling the bypass of the nearest town.

He had until noon tomorrow. A glance at his dashboard clock told him it was past four pm. He had tonight and the morning to kill six more people.

Shit. Kill six people?

The murder he'd just committed flashed across his mind in the most abhorrent of ways. His repeated stabbing was, in reality, a bad enough memory by itself, but the anxiety and terror that accompanied this memory made it worse; each mental recollection intensified the violence, enhanced the sounds of his knife's slick slicing, and increased the volume of Gus's agonising wails. Each slash of the blade felt tougher, each slice into the flesh deeper, and each squeal of Gus's pain felt like a symphony compared to the little whinges they had actually been.

He had just killed a man.

Brian. Had just. KILLED. A man.

Despite the faults in his character—the self-obsession, the narrowmindedness, the elevated sense of self-worth—he was not a psychopath. He still felt affection toward his sister, he felt love toward Lily, and, as he was just discovering, he may even have a smidgen of compassion for his fellow man that he was not yet fully aware of. He was capable of guilt. Remorse. Regret. And boy, was he feeling it now.

He ran his hand through his hair. It was drenched with sweat. His skin felt loose with heat, yet tight like ice.

He pulled up at a traffic light. The red light was Gus's blood; the passers-by enjoying their Christmas Eve were murderers with guns inside their wrapped gifts; and other drivers were angry bastards eager to knock him off the road.

"Get a grip..."

He needed to stop thinking about it.

Gus Phillips was a paedophile. A killer. A wretch. They had applauded Brian for what he did.

But he had still killed someone.

That changes a guy, doesn't it?

He put the radio on to distract his indistractable mind. It was a cover of an old Christmas song that was once popular and was now vaguely irritating, featuring some forgotten singer lamenting the follies of what happened last Christmas, and how they regretted it, and how they will act differently next year. Brian didn't care, he just wanted noise, something to distract him. His body was shaking and he could do nothing to stop it. Perhaps he was getting ill—or perhaps this was what killing a man does to you.

The song finished and the deejay spoke. "Happy Christmas Eve to all of you, and I hope you are enjoying it wherever you are."

Brian scoffed. Hardly.

"The forecast may be for rain tonight, but I know you will be warm wherever you are heading. Just turn up the volume, put on your slippers, sit back, and reminisce, because I've got you covered for the evening."

This guy was infuriating Brian. He went to change the station, then paused at the deejay's next sentence: "Except for you, that is, Brian—your Christmas Eve has only just begun."

His arms stiffened.

Had the deejay just said that?

I had to laugh. Honestly, the fucking idiot had no idea just what the ultimate ruler of Hell was capable of.

"That's right, Brian, enough of the Christmas classics for you—let's find out who's next on your Christmas list."

"Fuck you."

"Now, now, Brian, you don't want to aim such abuse at someone who controls your fate, do you?"

He stayed silent.

"Good boy. Now hold tight, keep driving until you reach the motorway, and we'll get to your next destination soon enough."

The traffic light turned green. He continued onward, then took a left off the bypass and followed the directions for the M5.

"Meanwhile, how about another annoying shitty classic?"

Just to torment him further, and for my own sadistic pleasure, I played another awful cover of a song about a person who only wanted a singular thing for Christmas— and that was *you*. Only, this remake was even worse than the original, with an unneeded falsetto and an extra bridge that added nothing but further seconds to a tedious tune.

Once he reached the motorway, the satnav came to life and revealed a route. He was to head north and get off in two junctions. Plenty of time for us to have another little chat.

He approached a car that was driving in the middle lane with no purpose for being there. The driver was not over-taking anyone. They were the most annoying kind of driver, and he undertook them in the slow lane to make that point, placing his middle finger at the window and wondering why it wasn't people like that who were facing eternal torment in Hell instead of him.

The song ended.

"And that was another shitty version of another shitty song. Now, let's discuss the target."

He huffed. Went into the middle lane to overtake a lorry, then returned to the lane on the left.

"Raised on the streets of Birmingham, this fellow grew to dislike the multicultural element of the city he lives in. He grew up with phrases uttered by his friends such as *Our City* and *Get Out My Fucking Country.* He would wear bomber jackets that his parents—a paediatrician and a primary school teacher—hugely disapproved of, and would go out with his friends to partake in an activity he called paki-bashing."

The satnav indicated that he was to get off at the next junction.

"As an adult, he joined the White Nationalist Party and protested against immigration and Sharia Law in the UK, despite being unable to name a single Sharia law. He partook in these protests across many cities, but these groups were not extreme enough for him—in fact, even the BNP and UKIP were not far-right enough for his agenda, and he was forced to create his own group, for which he became the leader."

With the junction approaching, Brian indicated left and joined the slip road.

"He has been arrested once, but that was not for his political demonstrations—it was for an assault on his wife, a charge he denied and which was later dropped. But we all know why that was, don't we? The fucker was guilty as shit, but his wife was afraid of what he'd do to her and their beautiful child if she said anything."

The satnav took him across a roundabout and a few miles down a country road. It led him to an estate full of large houses owned by the rich, each with lavish gates, huge drives, and a significant distance from the other houses. It made him feel sick that this bloke lived in such grand accommodation.

"The guy has a large social media presence and, although he has been kicked off most major platforms for his ideology, he remains on Twitter, where he is still allowed to push his rhetoric. Sometimes, people push back, and he is forced to unleash the identity of such people to his fans, who troll them until their lives are wrecked."

The satnav brought him to a stop outside the biggest house with the biggest gate and the biggest driveway. He pulled up the handbrake and killed the engine.

"That's right, Brian. You are to kill the cocky online influencer, millionaire and white supremacist, Spencer Dwight."

DEBT #2 SPENCER DWIGHT

THIRTEEN

S o many items in Spencer Dwight's house were made of glass. Glass tables, glass cabinets, glass ornaments, glass chandeliers, glass decanters, glass kitchen sides, glass shelves—even glass coffee mugs.

He loved it.

It made everything look expensive, and any time some nasty immigrant wormed their way into his house on a plumbing or electrical callout—such as they did, robbing good British folks' jobs and all—he would be sure to direct their attention to the fragility of items in his house, accompanied by the warning that they would pay for anything they broke from their measly but much appreciated wages or face a nasty bout of British aggression.

His other half was not made of glass, but that did not make her appear any less artificial. She was what society often referred to as a Trophy Wife—if that trophy was made of silicon and Botox. He was a man who appreciated things to be large, whether that was her tits or her lips or her arse, and he provided whatever money she needed to ruin her body in the pursuit of unachievable beauty. And, seeing as he had technically paid for about half of her body, he carried the belief that he owned her. And she never argued with such a notion. Of course she didn't. What would happen to her allowance, and her lifestyle, and her boob implants, if she objected to his ownership? She resented it, there's no doubt about that, but she resented it in dutiful silence, much as he believed his perfect Trophy Wife should. She was aware of the misogynistic rant that would follow any objections to the patriarchal balance of the household, and it wasn't worth the bruises she risked incurring.

Oh, how she *hated* him.

She really, truly, completely *hated* him.

Yet her parents loved him. He was rich and white—exactly the kind of man they had hoped she'd marry. But she would dream of days where she would spend dinner with a man who would listen to her; who wouldn't strut around the house like a peacock, with his feathers up and his hands in his pants; who wouldn't turn aggressive when he felt the slightest bit emasculated. He was a vile man who thought too much of himself and too little of others, and she wished that coping with his obnoxious personality wasn't the compromise she had to make to be rich.

Unlike his wife, his daughter still had hope of escaping him. At the tender age of eight, she was easily influenceable, but not yet completely influenced. She had a sweetness about her, a character that her teachers enjoyed teaching, and a prettiness that would make the public hugely sympathetic if she ever went missing. She adored her father, which made his temper hurt all that much harder, and she lived in fear of what might happen if she were to disappoint him.

In case you haven't figured it out yet, Spencer was an arsehole. The worst of all arseholes. An arsehole who never ceased spewing abhorrent shit out of his foul mouth—

usually shit about races he believed to be inferior; people ruining *his* country that he seems to think he has ownership of; and immigrants who, and I quote, "Come over here and steal our jobs, then don't even work."

Yes, he was thick, but being stupid didn't seem to matter when you were outspoken and controversial. He attracted other thick people who bought his crap, and they followed him online, and they would defend him to the death against anyone who dared to disagree with his comments. In fact, Spencer rarely had to defend the ideology that he frequently posted, as his fans would usually tear down anyone who dared disagree with an abusive brutality that would offend even the most hardened of objectors.

And while I am sure you are seeing a few links between Brian and Spencer—Brian was also rich as a result of being an online influencer—make no mistake, Brian may be a miserable prick, but Spencer was an indefensible, infuriating, racist, sexist, despicable bastard who loved how much he made people hate him.

Brian would never have a glass table in his kitchen. He loved the lifestyle but cared little about image. And he hated people because people were annoying, not because of their colour or creed.

In contrast, image was everything for Spencer—his wife, his house, his posts online; all of it was to portray the man he wanted people to think he was. And men like him never realise how wrong they are—they worship Donald Trump and vote for BNP and never have the intelligence to know that they are fucking idiots. After all, does it really matter if you're thick when you're too thick to realise how thick you are?

On this particular Christmas Eve, Spencer was drinking, as he usually did. He'd drunk a lot, but that didn't make him too disorientated; his body was accustomed to alcohol, and it took a lot to create any sense of dizziness. What might make a regular man pass out and wake up in a hospital simply gave Spencer the impetus he needed to carry on being a public nuisance. And whilst his daughter read her book (something he found strange, why would anyone read when you could go on your phone?), and whilst his wife tried to stay out of his way by sitting silently on the sofa, he sat back in his grand leather chair with a fancy lager balanced on his knee—if lager can ever be described as fancy—watching reruns of a daytime talk show where poor, uneducated people argued about trivial problems.

"I was thinking about popping out," his wife, Cassandra, said to him.

"Eh?" He didn't turn to look at her.

"I was thinking about maybe popping out, getting a few bits in for dinner, do us a nice buffet, what do you reckon?"

"Buffet? What the fuck you on bout?"

He still didn't avert this gaze from his mind-numbingly mediocre television show.

"Some food, babe. I thought–"

"Fuck that, I got some caterers comin' in. Just relax, av a beer."

"Well, maybe just popping out for a walk then, I thought–"

"Just fuckin sit dahn and shat up, would yuh?"

A moment of silence, and she spoke with the quietest, smallest voice she could, "But I was just thinking–"

"I said stay in the fackin haass!"

He didn't look around, but he could feel her fear. He relished it. He owned her.

She could walk out that door, sure she could, anyone could—but what then? What about her money? What about her liposuction? What about the reaction when she came back, how angry he'd be, how annoyed?

It wasn't worth it.

It was far better to just stay inside and hide her misery than it was to venture out that door and risk what he might do.

"I might get some wine from the kitchen then," she said, getting up and backing out of the room.

"Like I give ah fook."

She left the room as he laughed at the misfortune of a man on television. His daughter glanced up, then returned to her book. He grinned, satisfied with the control he exerted over the women in his house.

Meanwhile, outside the gates to the house where he was the king, a whimpering mess sat in his car, wondering how on earth he was going to kill someone like this.

This wasn't a loner like Gus.

This was a lad.

And Brian didn't know how to deal with lads.

They'd always been an enigma to him. A group of people who would laugh at him, who would shove him out of the way when they passed him in the school corridors, who would be loud and rowdy when they strutted through town in their football shirts.

And here was the biggest prick of a lad he had ever come across.

This imbecile was going to take some killing.

FOURTEEN

B rian readjusted his rear-view mirror until his eyes were looking back at him. He wiped sweat from his brow. Rolled up his sleeves. Rolled them down again. Shook his head, though he was unsure why.

"You've already done one," he told himself.

And he had.

He had done one.

Some greasy, disgusting fucker.

He'd stabbed him over and over.

Brian's conscience pricked at him, but Gus Phillips was a guy most would be pleased to dispose of. And this guy was just as bad. Spencer Dwight was a white supremacist, a wife beater, an idiot—he was the kind of guy who said awful things and spread hatred. He deserved it.

Yet Brian's trepidation was not down to whether Spencer Dwight deserved death; it was down to the practicalities of it, and how easy it would be to execute such a man. Brian had never met the man personally, but he'd seen Spencer online and in the news, and he'd seen the strut of toxic masculinity that clung to his stride with the stink of vulgarity. Spencer was a guy who was used to aggression, solved most of his problems with violence, and had an air of cockiness about him that made him seem impenetrable.

Brian would never admit to fearing anyone, but inside he felt sick; with a belly full of furious butterflies waging war with one another.

"Fuck it," he decided, and went to leave the car.

Then he stopped.

He'd almost forgotten to take his knife.

He rolled his eyes and shook his head. He was about to storm in there without a plan or a weapon and expect to have a chance! What the hell was he thinking?

He reached over to the passenger seat where the knife lay so prominently. Flickers of Gus Phillips' blood glistened on its steel blade, a reminder that Brian was becoming a serial killer.

Actually, that's not technically correct. A serial killer kills over a longer period. He was going to kill seven people in one night, which would make him a spree killer.

"Oh my God, does it fucking matter?" he demanded of his rear-view mirror image.

He wrapped his fist around the handle of the knife, flexing his fingers, his coarse skin feeling comfortable against the leather of the handle.

If he had done it once, he could do it again. But he needed a plan. He couldn't storm in there willy-nilly.

He scalded his reflection—he was meant to be a stone-cold killer, and stone-cold killers did not use expressions such as *willy-nilly*.

With a shake of his head, and forced gumption he didn't truly feel, he stepped out of the car and edged across the pavement. Even the ground was clean here, no litter or crumbs or discarded food—not even a leaf or a puddle; even nature protected the rich from untidiness. The bushes that lined the gates of adjacent houses were a rich green despite it being winter, and he wondered how it was even possible.

He put his hood up, aware of the potential for CCTV, and put his hands in his pockets along with his knife. He reached the large, extravagant gates of the Castle Du Spencer Dwight, and tried to push them open.

They did not open.

With a tut, he tried again, but still they did not open.

Reluctantly, he pressed the intercom.

"What?" grunted the respondent.

"Er... package... for Spencer Dwight."

"What is it?"

He shrugged. "Dunno."

A pause, and the gates opened. He entered the driveway, a symmetrical pattern of bricks across the ground, and passed a spotless white garage door. A BMW was on the driveway, and it looked cleaner than Brian's Mercedes.

He stopped at the front door. Paused. Looked up. Noticed the camera pointing at him. Turned back to the door, wondering whether he looked too conspicuous with his hood up. Finally it opened, and Spencer, clad in a designer tracksuit, gold chains, and a beer in his hand, stared expectantly at him.

Brian returned Spencer's stare, wondering what to do.

"Well?" Spencer said.

"Huh?"

"My fucking package? What, you waitin' to suck my cock first—where the fuck is it?"

"Oh, right. Yeah."

Wondering what he was supposed to do at this moment, he conceived of the ingenious plan of unleashing his knife from his pocket like it was the package and surprising Spencer by thrusting it into his heart.

"Yeah, it, er, it's here..." he said, gradually bringing his arm out of his pocket. Then, in a spurt of energy that Brian believed was unexpected, he shoved the knife forward and lurched toward Spencer.

Spencer stepped back with a bemused look, and Brian stumbled into the hallway.

Desperate not to lose the benefit of surprise—not that he ever had such a benefit—he swung the knife upwards. Spencer caught his wrist like a ball that was all too easy to catch.

"What the fuck is this?" he asked, looking at the knife in his hand. "Fuck, it's got blood on it! You tryin' to gimme aids?"

Brian tried to pull his arm free, but Spencer barely noticed the struggle. He tripped Brian by sliding his foot through Brian's ankles, twisted Brian's wrist until his hand was forced to release his weapon, then let go of the weak sod so he could hold the knife up in both hands and inspect it.

"This is fresh blood."

Panicked, Brian sprung to his feet and sprinted for the open door.

Spencer hit a button behind him, and the door shut and locked. Brain pulled on it, but it did not yield.

Suddenly, an eternity in Hell felt like it was going to get here sooner than expected.

"Please don't hurt me!"

Spencer laughed, and Brian tried to run past him.

Who knows why he didn't run in the opposite direction … He could have fled through the kitchen and, as unlikely as he was to escape Spencer's fortress, he would have at least given himself a few extra seconds of hope.

As it was, Brian tried to run past Spencer, and was unable to avoid the fist that Spencer lifted and swung into Brian's face.

Brian was unconscious before he hit the ground.

CHAPTER
FIFTEEN

I t was a lovely family Christmas. The fire crackled, Spencer's daughter half-watched a Christmas movie whilst playing Candy Crush on her iPad, and Spencer sat on the sofa with his arm around his wife, who was engrossed on her phone.

Oh, yeah, and they had a complete halfwit tied to a chair with duct tape in the corner.

As Brian came around, it didn't surprise him to see where he was or how he was bound. The oddest part of this situation was that Spencer's family didn't pay Brian much attention. Each ankle, each wrist, his waist and his chest were all tied to a retro wooden crossback dining chair, yet despite the presence of their captee, the guy's pre-pubescent daughter was more interested in her iPad, and his wife was more interested in finding the right filter for her selfie on Instagram.

"Eh eh, look hooz up!"

Spencer didn't change his relaxed posture; his feet remained on his fancy poof, his legs spread apart to display his crotch to the room, and his arm still draped around his wife (though not out of affection, but in order to show ownership, like a way of bragging to Brain, of showing that he was better than another man because of the attractiveness of the woman he could acquire—not that Brian found her fake tits and plastic face particularly attractive, but her generous cleavage and dress that rode the entire way up her thigh boasted of a sexual allure that Spencer was proud of).

Spencer did, however, mute The Grinch. His daughter didn't even seem to notice.

"Woz your name, bruv?" he asked. His diction was awful enough to offend the English language by itself, but was made worse by how fake it was. Spencer had been raised in a middle-class household, and despite being a huge racist, he seemed, at times, to be mimicking the sociolect of some sections of Asian culture. (I say 'at times' because there was little consistency to the dialect or sociolect he exploited—he just seemed to be happy so long as his speech was littered with grammatical inaccuracy, and that he sounded common enough that people would think he earned his privilege, and was not born into it.)

"B – B – B..."

"It starts wiv a B, that's good to know—what baht the other fackin letters?"

(See, even then, he said 'fackin' as if to imitate the cockney accent. This guy was such a tool.)

Brian's eyes widened as he noticed the M1911 pistol Spencer rested on his thigh. Not that Brian knew much about guns—he only knew the M1911 from Call of Duty.

"Brian."

"Brian! Stupid fuckin name."

Spencer sat up. Opened a small wooden box next to him, took out a spliff, and lit it. It stank like dark alleyways and the outside of nightclubs.

"Nah, Brian," he said, gun in one hand and spliff in the other. "You wanna tell me what a geezer like you is doing in my cribb, izzit?"

Brian tried to decipher what this man was saying, and could just about understand. He could not think of any decent answer, so he decided not to answer, though he felt immense pressure to do so.

"I mean, I get you is tryin to kill me an that, but you ain't even black or Asian or nuffin. So what beef yoo got with me?"

Brian sighed. He wanted to answer. He did. He just knew how ridiculous it sounded.

"Oi!" The shout made Brian's body jolt. "I asked you a question, izzit?"

"I—I was told to kill you."

"Now weez gettin somewhere, int we?" He took another drag on his spliff and relit it. "Now who is tellin you to kill me?"

Brian went to answer, but again realised how ridiculous what he was about to say sounded.

"You ain't no professional," Spencer continued. "Not with those bony as fuck arms. So who iz sendin a little boy like you to do me in?"

"The... The Devil..." Brian mumbled, barely audible.

"You what? Who?"

Brian took a breath, and said more clearly, "The Devil."

His wife looked at Spencer.

His daughter looked at Spencer.

Brian looked at Spencer.

Spencer paused, poised between bemusement and rage. As it was, he burst out laughing, almost manically, his laughter erratic and occasionally high-pitched. He wriggled in his seat, laughing too hard to stay still, and Brian wondered whether that was the first spliff Spencer had had today.

Then the laughter suddenly stopped. Spencer put out the spliff and stood. Brian would have shaken if his body wasn't bound so tight.

"I iz goin for a shit," Spencer announced, and sauntered up to Brian.

He bent over the cowering wreck, looked deep into his eyes, and almost choked him on the smoke that clung to his breath.

"An when I iz back, you better start givin me some answers, ye get me?" Spencer grabbed Brian's dick. "Or I iz goin to be choppin some tings off, yeah?"

With an intense, sinister glare, Spencer held Brian's gaze, and Brian could tell this guy meant it.

Spencer turned, walked away, up the stairs, and slammed a door behind him.

A silence lingered, broken only by the distant sounds of Spencer screaming at the pressure of his own shit.

Brian looked down and thought about what a fuckup he was. This was only the second guy, and he was tied up, about to be tortured to death. He only had until noon tomorrow to finish the hit list, and it was now—Brian looked around for a clock, but could not find one, so peered at the iPad the girl held in her hands—it was almost bloody midnight!

He looked down, huffed, wondered how long Spencer would prolong his torture before allowing him to die, then realised Trophy Wife was staring at him.

Brian stared back. He couldn't decipher the look. It was empty, like the woman was either stupid or unaware. After trying to decipher her expression for half a minute, he realised that she'd had so much surgery done that she couldn't form facial expressions anymore.

Brian tried to look away, but she kept staring, and in the awkwardness, he was forced to look back.

"Do you really want to kill my husband?" she asked. Her voice was bland and monotone, and Brian couldn't deduce in what expression or context she was asking this.

So he didn't answer.

She looked over her shoulder and said, "Quick, before he comes down. Do you really want to kill my husband?"

Brian returned her stare and, taking a gamble, answered, "Yeah. That was the plan."

She held his eyes for another moment. Brian noticed that the daughter still hadn't looked up from her iPad, and Trophy Wife didn't think this was strange.

In a sudden movement, Trophy Wife stood up, and he tried not to stare at her unnaturally massive breasts that never stopped jiggling. She crept toward Brian, keeping her eyes on the doorway, listening for noise from upstairs, until she reached Brian and leant over him. She wore so much perfume he struggled not to cough.

"He likes to untie people before he kills them, just so he can see them struggle," she whispered. She reached into her bra, shoving her hand right in, digging around, and withdrew a small but sharp blade. She reached around Brian, almost suffocating him on her bosoms as she did, and placed it in his right pocket. "That will be your best chance."

She stood, straightened her hair and, as she listened to the flush of the toilet from upstairs, returned to her place on the sofa, and resumed her former position.

CHAPTER
SIXTEEN

S pencer did not wash his hands. He was too rich to care about germs. So what if he got ill? He could pay for the best healthcare in the world. The doctors he could buy would suck gonorrhoea out of him should he be so unfortunate to catch it. Again.

Instead, he dragged his unwashed fingers across the sink and the wall and the door handle, and paused in the doorway as the toilet finished flushing (he'd left the door open to defecate). Then, in an impromptu moment of unrestrained self-love, he backed up slightly until he was in line with the mirror, and allowed himself the luxury of gazing upon his proud reflection. His self-admiration caused him to release a snort of mocking laughter at the difference between his handsome self and the idiot he had bound downstairs. He regarded his hard-as-nails face, the slick cobweb tattoo across his neck, and the sneer of defiance that scared so many people. The dweeb downstairs looked like he'd spent the last decade in Dungeons & Dragons chatrooms arguing over who was the best character in Star Trek, and it was almost an insult that an inept nerd such as this had the audacity to think he could inflict any kind of pain on a brute of a man such as Spencer.

And so, with one last supercilious grin at himself, he turned up his collar, readjusted his package, and strutted out of the bathroom and down the stairs like he was the cock that ruled the roost.

Oh, what a wretch Spencer beheld before him as he returned to the living room. Pathetic, small, and insignificant, in the middle of a room full of expensive objects that he best not get his blood over. It would probably be sensible to keep their prisoners in their basement, but not Spencer— he wanted this guy to see his house, wanted him to see his wife, and wanted him to see Spencer's expensive clothes and lavish lifestyle in the light—he wanted this guy to know that everything about Spencer was better than him.

"So," Spencer said. "Which part should ah remoov first?"

Brian glanced at Spencer's wife. She did not look back.

"Pretty, ain't she?" Spencer mused. "But a woman like that wun't fuck you, even if you had a ten-inch cock and a million quid."

Spencer stepped toward Brian, lifted his leg, and placed his boot on the edge of the chair between Brian's legs. The pathetic mess sweated like it was the high point of summer, and Spencer felt a little hard at the fear that he provoked.

He unleashed a knife from his sock. Small but lethal, with a rough leather handle. He placed it under Brian's nose, letting him smell the remnants of the dead, letting him feel the proximity of the silver.

Just as his wife had purported in secret, Spencer did not execute Brian immediately—he wanted to see his victim squirm, and he did not cut Brian yet. This was foreplay; the teasing before the climax. Instead, he flicked the knife beneath the tape that bound Brian's torso and dragged it slowly upwards. The tape clumped upwards before tearing, too thick to rip immediately, which relieved the pressure on Brian's chest and allowed the urchin to breathe a little better—for now.

Spencer could not help noticing another glance from Brian at his wife. She didn't look back, and Spencer felt a little perturbed—was he hoping for help? Hoping she would save him?

"She ain't gonna help you, you little dickhead."

Just to show his distaste at Brian's frequent glances, he penetrated his right shoulder by half an inch and dragged the blade down the side of Brian's torso. It was a thin scrape, not deep enough to enter his body, but enough to draw blood, a line of red sinking through his t-shirt.

Brian whimpered, and Spencer waited for him to utter whatever begs he wished to offer. But he did not offer any—something that spurred Spencer's aggression on even further.

He slashed the remaining tape from Brian's ankles and wrists in a fit of anger, and sent him to the floor with a heavy punch to the cheek.

Brian groaned, struggling, too weak to roll over, too pathetic to fight. His eyelids lolled, drooping, unable to fully open. His arms flinched, his muscles fought a heavy ache, his left hand clutched his wounded cheek, and his right hand rested beside his pocket.

Spencer kicked Brian's chest and pushed him over like he was upturning a plank of wood.

Brian's head dropped to the side, and he tried to mutter something, but it only came out as sparse, unintelligible syllables.

Spencer mounted the boy. Looked at his daughter,

hoping she would witness his display of dominance—she kept her eyes on her iPad—and lifted his fist high into the air.

That was when Brian's performance ended and the blade, tucked inside his fist, flew from his pocket to Spencer's neck in a swift movement that took them both by surprise. Spencer could not register what happened before Brian dug the blade into Spencer's neck again.

Brian swung his hand and hit Spencer in the face. It was more of a weak slap than a punch, but in Spencer's wounded state, it was enough to send him onto his side. Brian pushed himself to his knees then stabbed Spencer's belly and slashed his face and sliced his leg and kept slashing and slicing and slashing and slicing and slashing and slicing; it was a frenzied rage, one unmatched by even the wildest of carnivores.

You see, he wasn't just stabbing Spencer.

I mean, he was, but only literally.

Really, he was stabbing everyone who'd ever humiliated him—every lad who'd mocked him, every bloke who'd called him a puff for liking musicals, every bully who'd picked him last at PE class and ridiculed him for preferring computer games, every man who'd delivered offensive words under the pretence of banter.

Spencer was long dead by the time Brian ceased his slashing and slicing, and an ache had taken hold of his arm. The bloke lay in a bloody heap, a rag of clothes with a dead pillock inside, a corpse that would soon be eaten by mites.

Panting, he looked up.

For the first time, the daughter had lifted her gaze from the iPad, and the wife had turned away from the television. With the same empty faces, they looked at him.

Then his daughter said, blankly, "Thanks," before returning to her iPad.

He turned back to the body, trying to reconcile how this violent mess had been created by him, then stared up at Trophy Widow.

"You'd better go," she told him. "We have to call the police, but we'll give you a bit of time to get away."

Brian nodded.

Stood.

Looked again at what he'd done.

Fuck, did he do that?

And he bolted—through the hallway, to the driveway, over the gates, across the street, and into his car.

He glanced at the clock on the dashboard as he turned the ignition. It was well past midnight. He'd used half his time and was only two-sevenths through.

"Fuck!" he said as he spun the car onto the road and sped away from the estate.

He thought he'd feel more remorse, but honestly, he felt empty. He had done the world another favour—that we are all sure of—but his mind was stopping it from registering.

He wondered if each target would be so deserving of death.

Don't worry, dear readers. For the sake of our entertainment, I assure you they certainly will not.

CHAPTER
SEVENTEEN

B rian's foot weighed heavily on the accelerator as he directed the car out of the large, lavish estates and into the valleys, and did not intend to slow down.

After half an hour or so of aimless driving, he reached a single-track country lane. He continued along it at far greater speed than sense would allow, then stopped abruptly in a layby.

He hadn't passed a single soul in miles, but he hadn't noticed. His mind was elsewhere; a mess; full of poisonous thoughts; a contortion of twisting ideas, little of which made sense.

He punched the door open and tumbled to the ground. He was panting, almost hyperventilating, his breath rasping, struggling for air. He tried to rise from his knees, but an aggressive lurch of his body sent him back to the ground and a mouthful of empty vomit spewed onto the gravel below. He had eaten little all day, and it was mainly bile, and just when he thought he was done, his body lurched again and he projected another load over the ground.

He used the car to bring himself to his feet and

wandered away from the road, stepping through bushes that stabbed him with their twigs and into an open field. He stumbled onward, back and forth in a drunken motion, his vision lacking focus and his sense lacking presence.

He'd just killed two men.

Killed two men.

Killed. Two men.

He'd felt empty afterwards. He'd been pleased that he'd survived, and that he'd relieved the world of its most sordid bastards; the world would not miss Spencer Dwight, and neither would a family that was so eager to be rid of him. Despite how true that was, he still felt like his arm was holding the blade, was still swinging back and forth, was still slicing into flesh.

When his mind regained some clarity—not complete clarity, but enough that he could think—he made sense of where he was. He was in the middle of nowhere, with nothing but fresh night air to make the dry perspiration clinging to his skin turn cold.

He considered going back to the car, but sense told him not to. It would be tainted now. He'd fled the scene in it, and though he had his hood up, the car was probably caught on a procession of CCTV cameras guarding the property of the rich.

Would he go to prison?

The law doesn't forgive you for killing someone just because they were a dickhead. One could have murdered Hitler himself in the years preceding the European invasion, and they would still have been found guilty of the crime, despite the good it would have done.

He had to forget such thoughts.

Focus on this night.

Just get through it.

That was all.

Then he'd deal with such things.

Prison may be bad, but at least the people who ran it had some legal obligation to keep him safe, despite how much the prisoners would love a young-looking fresh face like his. Hell boasted no such morals. His torture would be for eternity, which was far longer than a prison sentence, and he must do all he could to escape that fate.

He knelt. His knees grew muddy, but it made little difference to the filthiness of his bloodstained clothes. He'd spent hundreds of pounds on them. They were hardly worth that now.

His mind drifted to Lily. Which was unexpected considering the predicament he was in, and the task he still had ahead of himself; nevertheless, his mind drifted to the one person in the entire world he cared for more than himself, and he wished he was sat with her now. His arm around her as she nestled into the dip of his shoulder. Reading some story to her, and doing voices that made her laugh, or maybe even putting together some kind of Lego kit he'd bought for her.

He always bought her Lego kits she already had, or that were completely inappropriate, and whilst Lily's parents groaned, she never did. She always pandered to Brian. Always told him it was okay, she'd just do the kit again, or give it a go. She never admitted that he'd bought her a crap present.

She was the only one who understood him.

And right now, he missed her.

And he wished he hadn't been such an arsehole to his sister. Even to her joke of a husband. That he could spend tomorrow afternoon with them. He'd be able to leave this world knowing that he'd made amends.

As it was, he knelt in mud with the blood of other men on his t-shirt and trousers, having been bound and humiliated, thinking about how pathetic he was.

He'd never let himself realise it before, but he did now.

He was pathetic.

So pathetic.

He'd always been pathetic.

And it hurt.

He looked up. Noticed something.

It was a doe. White belly with white spots over its brown back. It stood a few steps away, still, watching him. It surprised him that I'd send such a majestic creature, but he understood why it was there. He stood, straightened his back, and followed it, uttering no sound beside the grunts prompted by his lethargic mind and dishevelled body.

They wandered for a while, and whilst he knew he should hurry if he wanted to complete his task on time, he felt grateful for the rest that allowed his thoughts to reset, his body to let go of its tension, and his hazy mind to regain an element of awareness. Small flakes of snow fell from the sky, drifting along a small breeze and landing on the ground before turning to water, letting go of any sign they had ever fallen from the sky.

He'd heard that no two snowflakes were ever exactly alike, and he wondered if that was true.

He left the vast, open space of the fields and became submerged between tall trees that separated him from the moon's soft glow. Once trees were all he could see and no path was clear, the doe stopped. Looked back at him. Although it probably gave no expression, Brian couldn't help but feel it looked like a lost, wayward child beseeching a stranger for help.

As he stood there, illuminated by darkness, small pairs

of lights appeared in the thick black. He realised that these were eyes, and they belonged to owls, many of them, on branches of all the trees that surrounded him, casting their sinister glares on Brian.

One owl in particular stood out to him. It was the only owl that was on his level, rather than on a higher perch looking down at his weary, confused disposition. It focussed its eyes on his, held his gaze, and with that, provided him with the thoughts he needed to learn about his next target.

The man was in his twenties. He lived in the city centre. His name was Mitchell Myles.

His next question was how he would get to the city centre, but he needn't worry. Upon his next blink, I took the opportunity to pull his eyes closed and hold them there. By the time they opened, he was away from the grass and the owls and the doe and the trees and the fields.

Now, he was on a path next to a busy road that approached the city centre.

DEBT #3 MITCHELL MYLES

CHAPTER
EIGHTEEN

What kind of man would spend his Christmas night walking alone through the city centre streets?

In this question, I am not referring to Brian, who is ambling along the streets in search of the target—I am referring to the target himself. Mitchell Myles. A man who could easily be seen in two contrasting ways.

Some might refer to him as a father. Someone clever in what he did. Someone who loved his children and would do whatever he must to ensure they were fed.

Whereas some other more cynically realistic people might refer to him as a thief. A robber. A drug dealer. And for those who are familiar with the colloquial vernacular of certain locations of the UK—a chav.

On this particular night, on this particular Christmas Eve, he was wandering alone in search of partygoers and revellers to whom he might part with their money. He wore a tracksuit, entirely grey with two white stripes up the entirety of its left side; his short hair was greased to his scalp and forehead with copious amounts of gel; and he swayed from side to side with the walk of arrogance one might recognise in a bully. It was the strut of a man who believed the world owed him something; who thought that, if the world did not give him what he wanted, then he may take it by force.

But he did not seek to part strangers from their money because he was scum, or a waster, or a leach on society, like the rich elite may purport he was. He did it to provide his family with a Christmas. He married as a teenager, was a father before he turned eighteen, and was forced to drop out of his plumbing apprenticeship to find a way of better supporting his young family. His wife, a year younger than him, was sat at home, staring at a cheap Christmas tree with no presents beneath it—and Mitchell was determined to change that. He had a friend of a friend of a friend who had a shitload of toys that, or so they said, had 'fallen off the back of a truck.' If he could produce the funds this friend of a friend of a friend was demanding, then Mitchell could have free pick of those toys, and he could ensure Maya woke up in the morning with all the toys Santa Claus believed a good girl deserved.

But that meant getting money.

And that meant robbing people.

Couldn't he get a job? I hear you ask. Yes, I suppose he could. He could sit behind checkouts, or he could clean your offices, or he could serve your cheeseburgers. But why would he, when he could get more money by selling weed to his mates and taking money from strangers? Why would he give this up to take shit off rude customers when he earned more by refusing to play the capitalist game?

And no, he didn't feel guilty.

These strangers were richer than he was, and he cared little for what the departure of a few notes from their wallet would do to their lives. That iPhone in their pocket would get Mitchell a few hundred quid, which would put toys beneath the tree, which would subsequently brighten his daughter's face on Christmas morning—but it would be a brief inconvenience to the iPhone's owner. They would claim insurance, or simply buy another. It didn't matter that these may be honest people who worked hard and didn't have great financial means, as this narrative didn't fit his view. He told himself that they were rich, and told himself that his actions were not traumatic for the victims—and he believed it with the vigour of a person who did all they could to justify their unjustifiable actions.

He just loved his daughter. Of course he did. Don't you love yours? And he would do anything to see the smile tomorrow that, in his current state, he was unlikely to give her.

And so he traipsed through town, putting his hood up as he passed two officers sitting on the bonnet of their car sipping coffees from takeaway cups, keeping an awareness of who was around him and what they were doing. A woman, highly inebriated, sat on a bench with a stranger's arm around her, only a hotel room away from doing something she'd regret. A group of men, wearing smart shirts and ironed jeans, walked together with the banter of lads and the strides of private education. Middle-aged couples strolled down the street, the wives arm in arm like good friends, and the husbands forcing conversation as the only thing they had in common was the friendship of their wives.

Mitchel avoided groups. Crowds were okay, as you could get lost in a crowd and take a wallet in a hidden movement, such as an accidental knock against a shoulder, but a solitary group might notice what he was doing. So he kept walking, hands in pockets, through the sparsely occupied streets, passing more groups and more drunken couples and more people building the foundations of future regrets.

Across the street, he saw him.

A man. Maybe late twenties or early thirties, at a cash machine around the corner from an alleyway.

Mitchel hung back. Watched the stranger. Examined his clothes, expensive but poorly worn, and the way he held himself like a large child. He was hunched over, slouched like a timid boy, an easy target.

The stranger pocketed his cash, glanced over his shoulder, and turned down the alleyway.

Mitchel moved. Not running, but close to it. Walking with a jump in his step, entering the alleyway with a determination to get that money for his daughter.

Except, when he entered the alleyway, ready to gallop after the stranger, the stranger was not halfway down the alleyway as he expected; the stranger stood a few paces into the alleyway, barely visible in the shadows of the high brick walls.

The stranger—or Brian, as we know him—held out the cash he'd just withdrawn toward Mitchel.

"Here," Brian said. "There's about three hundred. Should be enough to get your kid something. Take it."

Mitchel scowled. How did this man know so much? Who was he? Why would he do this?

Mitchel snatched the money from the stranger's hand. Counted it. Shoved it in his pocket.

He would usually run away at this point, but he didn't. He was intrigued. For a reason he couldn't quite explain, it hurt his ego. The rush of the adrenaline wasn't there. The chase hadn't provided him with victory. He considered demanding the man's wallet and phone, just so he could reproduce the feeling of conquest.

Before he could do any of this, Brian stepped forward, his messy hair and bloodshot eyes appearing in the light.

"Can I buy you a coffee?" he asked.

Mitchel frowned. Unsure. This was too strange. He wasn't used to it.

"Come on," Brian said, walking out of the alley. "I know a place."

Hesitantly, Mitchel rechecked the money, ensuring it was real—it was—and he followed.

CHAPTER

NINETEEN

One might imagine that finding an open café in the late hours of Christmas Eve would be difficult. But, from the favour of fortune—or should I say, with a gentle nudge by myself—Brian knew the direction of such a café. A café that, before my influence, had been ready to close at 6pm.

The Devil works in mysterious ways...

Mitchel followed, not quite next to Brian, but not behind him either, unable to conceive of why he was so intrigued by this man. There was nothing about Brian that Mitchel could relate to. Brian's voice was that of someone who'd grown up in a sheltered middle-class upbringing; his walk was that of a nervous and unaware wanderer constantly seeking what he cannot find; and the general air about his being was that of a person who could not understand crime, as he had never experienced poverty. In contrast, Mitchel was a hard-nosed council estate kid who'd had to fight for everything. Their worlds were as far apart as two worlds could be, and Mitchel resented people like Brian. His favourite song was *Ill Manors*, purely because the lyrics ridiculed little rich boys like Brian who could never understand Mitchel's who, what, where, or whys. Every look he aimed in his new comrade's direction was dripping with loathing, consumed with displeasure, tantalised with disgust. He resented everything about this fragile fool.

Yet he could not help himself.

Usually, when Mitchel robbed a person, they shook or begged or quivered or pleaded or cried or ran. He'd never come across someone who was not only willing to part with the kind of money Mitchel needed, but handed it over with the offer of a warm drink on a chilly night.

The bell over the door announced their entry as they entered the café. Mitchel noticed the cheap, laminated menus, and pictures of greasy-looking food above the counter, and grumpy employees wiping down stained plastic tables with expressions that showed how little they wanted to be here. It wasn't the kind of place where the people working there pretended to enjoy customer service —it was cheap and direct, and there were no niceties needed.

As Brian ordered them a coffee, Mitchel became concerned that he was going to receive a lecture. Perhaps this was a man with wealth who wished to teach Mitchel a few lessons about how he lived his life; who wished to change Mitchel's life because he saw so much wrong with it. Mitchel had met these kinds of people in authority figures when he was an adolescent, such as teachers and police officers and social workers. Then, as he grew older, these people abandoned the belief that he needed to be saved; on the day he turned eighteen, he ceased to be a boy in need of help and became a burden on society.

Despite Mitchel's concerns, Brian did not start lecturing

111

him. Brian brought their coffees to a table, sat opposite, and simply opened the conversation with, "Cold night, isn't it?"

Mitchel grunted and warmed his hands on his coffee mug.

"I hate this day, don't you?" Brian asked, looking out the window, avoiding eye contact, like he was trying to seem less threatening to a predatory animal. At least, that's how Mitchel interpreted it. "There's so much pressure. So much forced happiness. I dunno, it doesn't feel worth it."

Brian lifted the coffee to his lips, sipped a little, then returned his mug to the table. Neither of them had removed their coats; it wasn't much warmer in the café than it was outside.

Mitchel went to respond, but didn't, feeling a wave of discomfort. He said, "I'm going toilet," then removed himself from his seat and marched across the café, searching for the symbol of the black man on the wall. He entered, avoided his reflection as he passed the mirror, and stood before a urinal.

As he peed, he looked around the wall in front of him, where front and back pages of newspapers had been pinned, assumingly to give urinators something to read. The papers themselves were weeks out of date, and the news that they displayed didn't interest him. He finished peeing, shook his cock a little, and zipped himself up. He washed his hands with water but no soap, left the toilets, and returned to his seat.

He stared at Brian, who stared back, and silence fell between them. They sipped their coffees without talking for a few minutes, until Brian finally said, "This is shit coffee."

Mitchel snorted a laugh. Brian was right. It tasted like plastic and swimming water and cleaning products.

"So tell me, mate"—the word *mate* sounded as unnatural from Brian's mouth as sex with the pope, but it was the only way he could think to relate to this man—"What's your deal?"

"My deal?"

"Yeah. Your deal. What is it?"

Brian sipped his coffee and watched Mitchel expectantly. Mitchel rolled his eyes, turned his head away, shook it, then turned back. His body had slid down the chair, his posture was slouched, and his legs were spread apart.

"Who says I have a deal?" he asked.

Brian had been doing so well. He'd offered a coffee, bought his company, and made idle chatter. Now he was talking in the exact way that would turn Mitchel away.

"People don't rob people in alleyways on Christmas Eve for nothing," he said.

Mitchel didn't answer. Not at first. He didn't have to explain himself to anyone, and he would not lower himself to this man's judgement. Even so, that British politeness that still existed within him made him feel that the price of a cheap coffee had been enough to buy his time, so he remained in his seat, downed his coffee, and waited to see if the conversation would change.

It didn't.

"I mean, why don't you get a job?"

"Eat shit, dickhead." Mitchel's body shifted from a slouched disinterest to leaning forward, and his head tilted like a bull about to chase after red—all so quick that it made Brian flinch and tense his muscles.

"Why don't *you* get a job?" Mitchel snapped.

"I have one."

"What?"

"I'm an online influencer."

"No, I mean a proper job. Why don't you get one of them?"

This stumped Brian. Honestly, he didn't desire set working hours and an arrogant boss any more than Mitchel did, but it was his wealth that made him believe his judgement had value.

"Fine, I'm sorry," Brian said. "Let's just finish our coffee."

Mitchel punched his empty polystyrene cup as he stood, sending it flying across the café.

"Fuck your coffee," Mitchel spat, lurching over Brian.

He strutted out of the café with a lingering scowl, carrying his cocky hardman attitude in the sway of his heavy body. He had the money he needed, and it was time to get the toys he needed. He didn't know why he'd given this guy any time to begin with. It was like something possessed him. They were as different as two people could be, and did not belong at the same table.

He sauntered down the street without looking back.

TWENTY

B rian watched out the café window, able to see far across the high street from his perfect position. He'd never put bleach in someone's coffee before, and he was unsure how long it would take to kill someone, and he'd only put a little in as he didn't want Mitchel to taste it—but surely it couldn't be long?

He considered googling it but had watched enough true crime documentaries to know that, should he be identified as a suspect in Mitchel's murder, the police would use such searches as evidence. Instead, he relied on his own beliefs, as uneducated and presumptuous as they were, and estimated it might be an hour or so.

As it turned out, it was almost instant.

He watched keenly as Mitchel swaggered down the street, walking with an arrogance that Brian had attempted but never quite mastered, and felt a wave of relief as Mitchel grabbed his belly and fell to his knees. Brian imagined the pain would be intense, the bleach burning from the inside, with a feeling of inescapable nausea accompanied by self-deprecating fury as Mitchel realised he'd fallen for such a simple trick.

Yet, as well achieved as this execution was, it felt different to the others. Brian didn't feel quite as justified in the killing of Mitchel Myers.

Mitchel was a criminal, yes, and had caused many people distress on many occasions. He thought his crime would only be an inconvenience, and gave no thought to the trauma he caused a person by robbing them at knifepoint. Even so, his intentions were different. He wasn't a thoughtless molester-murderer high on his own ability to commit his crimes with no consequences like Gus Phillips, and nor was he a conceited drip on the world who abused his family and brought hate to minorities like Spencer Dwight. Regardless of the immorality of his actions, this was a man doing all he could to provide for his family and avoid his child growing up in poverty. Whilst Brian felt little regret from the execution of his first two targets, this time he felt a huge sting of remorse. It wasn't just in his mind; it was also a physical pain, his belly hurting like he had been the one who ingested bleach, and his legs shaking like they were not under his control, and his brow perspiring like he was wearing an anorak in a sauna.

Still, Brian kept watching his target, waiting to confirm the kill.

Mitchel brought up a little sick, but not much. Not enough to remove all the bleach. Or so Brian hoped. At least, he thought he did. His instincts were at war with his intentions; he felt an urge to walk over and help Mitchel, to call him an ambulance, and to provide reassurance that it was all going to be okay.

Mitchel's body was lurching. He was rolling on the floor. Writhing. Squirming.

It surely wouldn't be long…

A pair of women were walking past, arm in arm, laughing about something or other, and noticed Mitchel struggling on the ground. They stopped and asked if he was okay. For a moment, his torment paused, and he looked like he was about to look at them and respond—but he didn't. Instead, his red face lifted, and he set his glare on Brian.

Brian decided it was time to leave, fearing he might be identified as the culprit. He finished the last sip of his coffee, stood, zipped up his coat, and marched out of the café, turning the corner so he was out of sight of Mitchel's suffering.

The satisfaction of a job well done was a distant feeling in his mind, overshadowed by a pang of tears he felt pushing at his eyes. He hadn't cried since he was a child, and he couldn't quite understand why the tears were coming now, but here they were, pushing through the prison bars of his self-deception, glistening his cold cheeks with evidence that he was human after all.

He stopped in a car park, ending a stride that lasted fifteen or so minutes, and leant against the door to a public toilet that had been locked many hours ago. He punched the door and screamed, his voice echoing around the sparsely occupied car park with no one there to hear it.

Except for me, of course.

"Oh my," I said, leaning against the bonnet of a BMW that had frozen over with ice. "You are having quite the night."

He turned to me and scowled. He wanted to say *fuck you*, but he didn't, because as conflicted as he was, let's be honest, who's going to say fuck you to a creature who holds their fate in their claws?

"Are you enjoying yourself?" I enquired.

His glare grew so intense that it made me a little aroused. "Are you?"

"Oh, yes, quite. It has been an evening I will look back on for years to come."

He shook his head, wiped his cheeks, and shoved his hands in his pockets. He rested his weight on one leg, raised his eyebrows, and looked at me with the look his mother used to give him when he hadn't brought his dirty plates downstairs.

"Who's next?" he asked, with an air of despondence I enjoyed.

"Excuse me?"

"I said, who's next? Who's the next target? Let's get this over with."

"Oh, dear Brian, that is not how this works."

"What do you mean? You tell me who, I do it. I don't have much time, are you trying to delay me further?"

"I would do no such thing. But for you to be given the next target, you need to have actually killed the previous one."

"What are you on about? I put bleach in his coffee. He's dead."

"Dead? Did you see him die?"

"I saw him in a lot of pain."

Realisation came upon Brian like a monster creeping up behind him.

"Mitchel Miles is not dead," I stated, enjoying the sight of painful realisation overcoming his downtrodden visage, unable to stop myself from sniggering. "Right now, he is in an ambulance, on the way to the hospital, with the company of two women who sought emergency care. Did you honestly think a few drops of bleach would be enough to kill someone?"

Brian closed his eyes and shook his head. "Fuck."

In a stroke of kindness quite unnatural to my character, I held out a needle filled with poison and suggested that it would be enough to complete the mission.

CHAPTER
TWENTY-ONE

T he two women were oh so distressed, almost fulfilling the misogynistic trope created by centuries of literature of weak-willed women becoming hysterical over the stimulation of their emotions. Truth is, they were acting as any non-psychopath would when coming across a man suffering, close to death, in agony, and were empathetic enough to accompany a man in distress to the hospital.

Once he entered A&E, the women were at a loss of what to do. Despite it being the late hours of Christmas Eve, and both of them needing a good night's sleep in order to address a stressful day with their families in the morning, they remained in the waiting room until the man's family arrived. Eventually, someone arrived, saying he was this stranger's brother.

The women were sceptical.

This man was so different from the man they had accompanied to hospital.

He walked with a timidness prompted by years of middle-class repression, with a wariness prompted by unsureness, and with an eagerness that struck them as too eager.

Still, they left—but not until they'd given this man a hug as a way of emptying themselves of the compassion that had been pricking at them for the past few hours. They directed him to where his brother was being treated, then searched for the exit, shaken by the experience.

Brian, the man who had announced himself as the stranger's brother, was glad to see them go. He was torn between admiring their kindness in helping a stranger, or being struck with frustration at their hinderance. Once they had disappeared around the corner, he crept through the hospital corridors.

He didn't actually need to creep, but Brian didn't realise that. He had never been to a hospital before, not even for a sick relative or a broken bone, and he had expected to be questioned by someone about the purpose of his presence, perhaps by a nurse or security guard. As it was, he walked freely through the hospital, undisturbed by health workers rushing from one part of their job to another, each under too much pressure from a strained NHS to notice a stranger carrying poison in a needle.

He came upon the cubicle where Mitchel was being treated and, finding there was still a doctor and nurse with the patient, stood back and watched from afar. There was a water cooler against the wall a few steps away, so he took a plastic cup and filled it, sipping on it, taking his time, giving a reason for his being there.

It appeared they had been forcing Mitchel to be sick and were wiping the last dregs from Mitchel's mouth as he laid unconscious. After they were sure he had finished bringing up the contents of his stomach, they parted from Mitchel for a few minutes to cater to the demands of an extortionate quantity of patients that meant they could not dedicate enough of their precious time to such a man who'd been on the brink of death.

This was Brian's opportunity.

He approached Mitchel's body, checking the corridor was clear, still perplexed to find himself unquestioned. He stood beside Mitchel and pulled the curtain around the cubicle to give him some privacy. He waited to see if anyone objected, but he didn't even hear a single footstep. Content that they were alone, he turned to the man that lay unaware in the bed.

Mitchel looked peaceful. It's a cliché to say it, but that was how he looked, and it was a huge contrast to the arrogant criminal he'd appeared to be when he was swaggering around town. As Brian took the needle from his pocket, he almost stopped himself, considering the act to be selfish, aware that he was taking a father's life to save his own.

Who was to say where Mitchel would end up?

With the acts Mitchel had committed, would he end up spending an eternity in Hell?

Mitchel's fate was not Brian's problem. Still, he couldn't help thinking of the fate of Mitchel's family.

His daughter would learn to hate Christmas. The day would come around every year, and for the rest of her life, Christmas lights and tinsel would prompt a memory of how it felt to wake up on Christmas morning with anticipation of Santa's visit and presents under the tree, only to be given the gift of death and a life without a father. When she grew up and had kids, would she be able to encourage them to enjoy Christmas? Or would she be forever damaged by the pain she'll find when she wakes up?

Then again, was she better off without him?

Without his influence, did she stand a better chance of

not ending up a criminal herself? Was her mother a woman of more integrity than her husband? Would she raise her daughter to be a better woman without the toxic guidance of a father who would rather rob strangers who work hard than work hard himself?

He ran his thumb over the end of the needle, the part he needed to press to bring *The End* to this man's presence in this world.

With a sigh, he decided these decisions were not his to make. He was a soldier, and it was his job to do my bidding, and it was not up to him to choose whether his target was worthy of death.

He pushed Mitchel's head to the side, only slightly, and exposed the man's neck. He placed the tip of the needle against it, ignored his better judgement, and pressed upon the syringe.

The needle unleashed poison into Mitchel's body.

Except, it actually didn't, did it?

I mean, if you really think I gave Brian poison to inject into Mitchel's body, then you clearly do not know how I work.

Brian stood back, expecting death to begin its process, readying himself to leave when he was sure.

But Mitchel didn't die.

In fact, the exact opposite happened.

Following the vast quantity of adrenaline Brian had just injected into Mitchel's body, his eyes opened wide with an intake of breath, and he sat up, suddenly alert.

CHAPTER
TWENTY-TWO

"*What the fuck!*"

Brian had never witnessed someone move so rapidly from a state of comatose absence to urgent malice.

I have witnessed such a sight in my eternity of induced suffering, especially after the insertion of a particular implement into a particular orifice—but, being of mortal descent and not being fortunate enough to have experienced the wonders of torture and fatalities that devils and demons get to relish in, Brian was alarmed to see Mitchel's face become so suddenly vigilant.

Brian did what any pathetic human would do, of course —and I deem all of you reading this to be a pathetic human (don't think you're any better because you claim to own some kind of morality that others don't)—and he reacted instinctively.

On this occasion, that was to smother Mitchel with his pillow.

His bleeping heart monitor picked up pace, but Brian

traced the wire of the machine to the plug in the wall and pulled it out before it could alert anyone.

Mitchel struggled and, under normal circumstance, would have been able to remove Brian's sorry attempt at pillow-induced asphyxiation from his face—and he would have followed it by, as I have heard you humans say, *Kicking His Arse*—as it was, he was weak and unable to react quickly enough, and his body was still recovering from trauma, and he was still groggy despite how quickly he'd left his comatose state. Despite this, Brian still pressed all his weight onto the pillow, pushing down with his arms and his torso, using every bit of energy his body could muster.

Mitchel's arms thrashed a little, pulling at Brian's arms, but were too weak to stop him. Still, if movies have taught you that this process is quick, then you will find yourself quite surprised at how long it takes for someone to suffocate to death. Even once Mitchel lost consciousness—which he finally did—Brian did not accept this as the end. Not after the folly of the bleach debacle. He kept the weight of his body pressed upon his target long after he thought it was done, ensuring that the guy was dead before he could move onto the fourth target.

He kept looking over his shoulder, glancing at the curtain, waiting for it to twitch. Much to his good fortune, it didn't. The doctors and nurses were busy with other patients from their monumentally high patient load and, whilst in ideal circumstances they would have been back to check on Mitchel Myles, the strain put on the NHS was, in this case, beneficial to Brian's probability of success.

Eventually, after some long minutes had passed, Brian allowed himself to relieve the pressure he was putting onto the pillow and to stand back. He waited for a flinch of the arm or a twitch of the body, but it was not forthcoming. He took the pillow from over Mitchel's face and surveyed the man's state.

He tried to feel for a pulse in Mitchel's neck but, being honest, he had no idea where on the neck to find it. Instead, he moved his hand over Mitchel's mouth and felt for breath, of which there was none. Then he put his hand over Mitchel's heart and felt no beat.

He was confident it was done.

He placed the pillow beneath Mitchel's head, left him comfortably dead, and edged toward the curtains.

He peered out.

There was a nurse in deep discussion with another nurse down the corridor to his right, holding a small polystyrene cup filled with what Brian assumed must be coffee. Her hair was frizzy and there were sweat patches beneath her armpits; the remnants of a long shift in a thankless job operating under constant pressure.

To his left, there was a vacant corridor that turned to the right after approximately twenty feet.

Ensuring his hood wasn't just up, but was also tucked over his face, he turned to his left, put his hands in his pockets, and walked away, not so slow as to hang around, but not so fast as to attract undesired attention.

The hospital was like a maze and he ended up leaving through a different exit than the one he'd originally entered. It didn't matter. He was out, and he was back in the city, and could continue his onward journey through the nighttime streets where no one else remained.

He checked his watch. It was approaching four. He was tired, but despite this, he was alert, eager to get going on the next target.

Even so, he needed a break after such excursions. So I

gave him one. I let him walk and get this kill out of his system before I delivered his next name.

Then, in the relief of a few minutes free of murderous intent, I found it funny to see him crying.

This was more than just the few tears he'd fought earlier —this time, it was like thunder, like a tempest from his eyes, and he did not try to hide it. There was no one else around, and even if there was, people kept themselves to themselves at this time of night. So he allowed it, unaware of the humiliation he would feel if he knew I was still watching him so intently. He let it come, streaming, pouring, punching its way into reality, screaming liquid life into the world. He made sounds too, like a child does when they want a parent to hear that they are crying, like a dying animal caught on barbed wire. I laughed, and I let some of it carry across the icy breeze and onto his cold cheeks where his tears turned to ice.

He didn't care.

He carried on crying.

Until I decided it was enough.

And I directed his aimless wandering toward the edge of the city, past the advertising signs displaying last year's products, past the graffitied walls of anonymous gang signs, past the parked cars covered in frost waiting to be vandalised.

An hour passed as he wandered into the suburbs. The sun showed no sign of rising—not yet—and he came to an estate where middle-class families would be tucked up in bed, their doors locked to keep the bad people out.

I waited for him on a bench in the middle of a green where children played during the day. He noticed me there and, without lifting his head, wiped his eyes on his thick coat sleeve and perched on the edge of the seat. He looked to his feet, listening to the silence of the cold reality of the night, and I watched as this broken wreck of a man tried to stop himself from crumbling.

Once he was ready, I gave him the name of Allison Archer.

DEBT #4 ALLISON ARCHER

TWENTY-THREE

A lison stretched her back. Rubbed her eyes. Looked at the clock and held her stare, her tired mind not quite registering the numbers.

5.48 a.m.

It was early. Too early. The kids would be up for Christmas morning soon, perhaps in just over an hour, but for now, the house was at rest. Her husband, the great Doctor James Archer, slept soundly beside her. His snore was loud and obnoxious, and even after twenty years of marriage, it still made her muscles prick with rage. There could be a storm outside, the likes of which came attached to a natural disaster, and his snore would drown it out with an ease that would be tough to define.

She struggled to remember who this man was when she'd met him at twenty years old. There was so little of him left. But that was fine; she could cope with losing him. What drove her crazy—what really riled her—was that when she looked down at her own arms, and her own legs, and her chest, and her feet, she struggled even more to remember herself.

She wasn't the only one whose body had shown the signs of entering her forties. His had too. And it wasn't just the obvious signs of ageing that she resented about him—the rounder belly, the grey hairs, the groans as he sat down—it was the subtler aspects that disgusted her. The extra-long nostril hairs; the way his chewing had become louder; the way he always surveyed a crossword in the evening with an air of defeat, rather than an air of potential triumph.

She had acquired such similar negative aspects, and she was aware of it. Perhaps too aware. She was less tolerable of how long he took to answer a question; she was less patient when her child couldn't think of the right word; and she struggled to get aroused by her husband at all. To be honest, she'd never really seen sex as something to cure her arousal, but to cure her insecurities. Being undressed made her feel wanted. Being used made her feel loved. Being fucked made her feel purposeful. Her age was taking all those reassurances away from her.

And that, my friends, was the real reason Allison woke up at 5:48 a.m. She'd pass it off as her needing the toilet; it was a simple explanation for why she directed herself to the ensuite. But that did not explain her eagerness to lock the door and be as silent as she could, nor did it explain why she took her phone with her, and nor did it explain why she kept staring at the door as she texted *him*, as if James was going to kick it down and demand to know what she was doing.

James was still asleep. Her children were still asleep. The entire world was still asleep. All except her, and the man at the other end of her text messages. The one whose notifications were muted.

His words were so passionate. So keen. So needy. So full of desire.

There was no romance to them, but she was old enough to know that such a concept wasn't real—or that, if it was, it was only used to persuade a woman to be willingly fucked, and not out of any desire to make her genuinely happy. But she didn't care. His text messages were so feral, so animalistic; he was so vehement when he said he wanted her, needed her, now, right now, as if the world was going to implode if he was unable to roll up her dress and fuck her from behind.

He was using her. He wanted one thing. But she didn't mind, because she was using him too, and she only wanted one thing: except whilst he wanted a fuck, she wanted a sense of self-worth. It was a reciprocal toxicity, and they both got what they wanted from the other.

She texted back with the words he wanted to hear. Words that conveyed how much she wanted him to take her, that she couldn't stand having to go through this day with her husband, that she was oh so desperate for the next time he would be inside her. Then she'd wait, eager with anticipation, for the next reply to arrive and give her a boost of happiness that would temporarily ease her self-loathing.

Such an alleviation didn't last long.

It was like any drug, and the high left as quickly as it arrived. Once her addiction had been catered for, she needed greater amounts to feel the same rush. So she'd say whatever she needed to prompt his dirty talk again, and the more descript she was, the more she pushed away her repulsion and prioritised his needs.

Someone wanted to fuck her. Even though she was a mother. And married. And had an ageing body. And was no longer desirable. And was no longer useful to society.

She knew her body wasn't the steeple it had been in her youth, and had become a decrepit, old church, with its grand architecture covered in moss, and its stained-glass windows blurring what was inside.

But someone actually wanted that body.

And, despite how much James might still perform desire, the fact that another man wanted it with a carnal need, and not out of the necessity to maintain a marriage, was incredibly self-aggrandising. She relished every word, reading the texts over and over, avoiding looking down at her wobbly breasts that dangled helplessly without a bra, and her vagina that felt looser than it once was, and her belly that bore stretch marks that her love for her children could not forgive.

It was her life.

It wasn't a great one, but it was hers.

Even so, she wasn't a paedophile, a murderer, or a thief like Brian's previous targets.

Centuries ago, an adulteress would have been seen as worse than such people. They would have been whipped, or mutilated, or put to death. But, as much as I enjoyed those days, they are long gone, and an adulteress is really just someone who is unhappy, or someone who is attempting to reclaim what was once theirs.

And so she offered her body to a man she barely knew.

She didn't need him to promise her forever. She didn't even need him to promise her tomorrow. Love was not a prerequisite for this exchange. She just needed him to promise her of his desires, and to give value to her sexuality.

The explicit and descriptive nature of the words and pictures he sent made her feel useful again.

And that made her pity herself most of all.

TWENTY-FOUR

T he bathroom light wasn't on, but Brian could still see a faint light in the window, like a mobile phone screen shining on the mirror.

He stood outside, beneath the branches of the tree, hidden in shadows cast by long, thick branches. He watched the window, trying to justify what he was about to do, trying to find some logic that would make this murder okay.

I could tell this was going to need my influence. Whilst Brian's sense of self-deception was strong, there was still too much doubt. I needed to replace it with an unhealthy dose of willingness and resolve.

*The whole world lies under the sway of the wicked one—*John 8:44.

He knew Allison was in there. He knew this because I wanted him to know. And he knew she was alone, in the early hours of the morning, texting a man she'd easily succumbed to, who she'd let plough her in hotel rooms, a man who got dressed within five minutes of ejaculating on whichever part of her took his fancy.

Allison would always leave the hotel room after him, but she didn't care.

Brian's instinct was to ask—did she not realise she was being used? But that's not the point, is it? Because whilst her bit on the side was after was a quick fuck, something easy and non-committal, something that reinforced the notion that his gender was nothing but a bunch of predatory pricks drawn to a woman's cunt like zombies to brains —she was using him too. He treated her like an object, but she wanted to be that object, and in that way, he was a victim just as much as she was.

And yes, I know large portions of the female population will cry out in outrage at such a suggestion, but I don't care. I'm The Devil—I don't give a fuck.

But just because she was using him, and being used in return, it did not make her a bad person.

At least, not to Brian.

Brian knew many religious zealots and old-fashioned folk who would find adultery disgraceful—but to Brian, it was the least bad thing on the list. Hell, he'd fucked a woman or too who was married, or in a relationship, or was unhappy and drunk and looking for an antidote to cure their misery; a remedy Brian had been keen to offer. But he had never, ever, ever seen any of these women as bad people.

Confused? Yes.

Promiscuous? Let's not judge.

But evil? Bad? Deserving of death?

Hell, no!

He'd seen them as part of an exchange, people whose infidelity came out of chronic unhappiness, or people who lived in a world where monogamy was an unhealthily reinforced societal construct that was more difficult to adhere to than you'd like to admit.

For this reason, Brian concluded that Allison did not deserve to die.

The others, maybe, you could make an argument that the world would have less pain in it without them. For each target he'd dispatched, despite the grave regret and inevitable trauma that followed, he could at least convince himself that they deserved it. But not this woman.

She was a mother. That was clear. He didn't need to see her kids, he could surmise as much from other obvious clues —the people carrier on the driveway, the amount of presents under the tree that he could see through the living room window, the abundance of Christmas lights on the exterior of the house clearly intended to excite a younger audience.

And for all Brian knew, Allison could be a great mother.

He shoved his hands in his pockets. Looked down. Shook his head. He could not do this.

But then what?

Would he face an eternity in Hell?

Would Allison?

He was an atheist, but seeing The Devil on several occasions had made him question his beliefs. And, if religion did exist, as it must if I am to exist too, then the texts have been pretty clear on religion's attitude toward adultery. In fact, didn't it specify it in one of the ten commandments?

Allison would face the fate that he was trying to avoid, and it would be he who put her there.

But what was the alternative? It was her or him.

Many of you might say, *Well I'd choose me*, in which case, fuck off you sanctimonious arse!

Really?

You would take an eternity in Hell to save a stranger?

Get a grip.

I'm not talking about a mild discomfort here. You wouldn't just receive a minor blow to the head, or a kick in the shin, or the simple loss of your life. You would spend the rest of the eternity being force-fed your own spleen, anally raped with the claws of my most revolting demonic princes, repeatedly impaled with the sharpest of objects, and set on fire without the sweet relief of death, left to burn and scream as we laugh—and that's just the start!

Throw them into the blazing furnace, where there will be weeping and gnashing of teeth—Matthew 13:50.

If you insist that you would inflict eternal torture and damnation on yourself to save someone else, you are lying —not to me, but to yourself.

Humans always look out for themselves in the end. It's how you evolved. It's in your evolutionary psychology. It's all about survival. And right now, this was about Brian's survival, and he knew he had no choice.

He looked over his shoulder, like he expected me to be there. Like I would appear and talk him through it, or offer an alternative, or be there to reassure him.

But he couldn't see me.

I was there, but the limitations of his human perception would not let him see what was right before him. My whispers would be silent inside his mind, and my touch would feel like a breeze against his skin, and my hatred would be the nausea churning in his gut; I would be an absent hand guiding him that he never felt or noticed.

With a shaking arm, he pushed sweaty strands of hair away from his face. He was burning up, hot, sweaty, yet he was shaking like he was cold. His body quivered, yearning for something to save him. He might be getting ill. Or he might already be sick.

He trudged onward, approached the back gate, reached over, and pulled the bolt across. With a glance back, he entered the garden.

Just as he began seriously considering how he was going to do this, he was alerted by a lump in his pocket. He shoved his hand inside it and brought out a phone.

Allison's text messages appeared on the screen.

It was the phone of her secret friend.

And it was unlocked.

And no, it hadn't appeared by magic—this was a helping hand from myself, being the kind, gracious bastard that I am.

Come outside, he typed, and sent.

Then he backed away from the garden doors and retreated to the shadows.

You became filled with violence within, and you sinned— Ezekiel 28:16.

This was when I let him think he was in control, and I hovered above him like a puppeteer, keeping him unaware of The Devil's sway.

CHAPTER
TWENTY-FIVE

*C*ome outside.

Outside?

Allison looked around, seeking confirmation she was alone. The same dark tiles she'd chosen with her husband glared grimly back at her. The shower curtain was a lump of shadows, and the kitchen tap gave an occasional drip; the kind of vague, ominous noise a prisoner in a basement might hear.

To the garden.

Now.

She stared at the mobile phone. If her husband dared to make such a demand, she would reply with fury; when her man made such a demand, she found his directness hugely arousing. It excited her and terrified her.

I am waiting.

She glanced at the door. What if her husband looked outside? What if he saw them? What if he found out and Christmas morning was ruined? The angel on her shoulder begged her to choose her marriage, to choose monogamy, to choose the right way.

She disregarded the angel with a shrug.

She *loved* that he might catch her. And not because she wanted to be caught, because she certainly did not; the affair was too good to ruin with her husband's interference. It was because she desired the danger, the risk, the excitement. It turned her on to undermine her husband. She'd fuck her man amongst the bushes her husband planted and the thorns would scrape her skin and the pain would let her know she was still alive. His cum would drip down her leg and mix with the blades of grass and bless the garden with another man's seed. She would watch her husband water that garden in the summer as she grinned, chuckled, licked her lips, moist as a wet napkin.

She stood up. Considered flushing the toilet to give the impression that she had been in here to make use of it, but decided against it—she could still hear her husband's booming snores, and she did not wish to wake him. She left the ensuite and tiptoed across the bedroom, the carpet soft on the soles of her feet. She opened the bedroom door slowly to silence the creak, stepped into the hallway, and closed the door behind her.

She crept toward the stairs. Paused. Looked toward her son's room. The door was ajar. She edged toward it, paused in the doorway, and watched him sleep. He was beautifully clueless, a perfect little man. Would he grow up to be a bastard like the rest of them?

She closed her son's door and crept down the stairs.

She squinted as she approached the garden doors, trying to find his face in the darkness—perhaps in the shadows of a tree, or behind a shrub, or on a bench.

Nothing.

Except...

A figure. In the darkness of the distant bushes, the black

of the night concealing his face and covering his body in shadow. She couldn't see him, but she could see his outline.

She opened the doors, stepped into the garden, and opened her mouth to speak—then her phone vibrated.

Stop there.

She stared at her phone.

And she did as she was told.

Take two steps forward.

She looked up at the figure and obeyed.

Good girl.

She smiled. She liked it. It made her feel naughty. This entire situation was like a fantasy she hadn't even thought of. He remained disguised by the night, unknown to her, instructing her. She tilted her head to the side in the playful manner he had become used to.

"What now?" she asked, her voice singsong and hushed. She bit her lip, hoping he would ask her to do something terrible.

Turn around and bend over.

She giggled. Turned around. Bent over. Allowed her nightie to creep up, exposing the base of her buttocks, not ashamed to show him the wrinkles at the top of her thighs; he always said he was most attracted to her imperfections.

She raised her eyebrows and smiled over her shoulder. It was her sexy smile—or as sexy as she felt it could be.

There was a movement in the shadows. It was his hand. It was moving. Quickly. He was masturbating. Over her.

God, it made her feel good.

Take it off.

She raised her eyebrows. "Are you not going to ask nicely?"

Now.

She glanced up at her bedroom window. Any moment

now those curtains could open. Her husband could look out. He could see her.

And so what if he did? To hell with him!

She removed her nightie with a sly smile. Slowly. As if to tease him, to be coy and seductive – but they both knew how keen she was. She was struggling to contain herself. It wasn't just the taboo nature of what they were doing; it was the way he desired her. The way he was jerking himself over her body. The fact he even wanted to jerk over her body. She'd have found a man doing this repulsive in her twenties, sickened as she was by the constant sexual harassment her younger self endured—now, she felt so unwanted that she didn't mind being reduced to an object of lust.

Face me.

She turned around. Stood. Naked, two steps into her garden.

There were no lights on in her neighbour's windows. She kind of hoped they were there, wanting her, craving her, enjoying the show.

He threw something from the darkness, and it landed at her feet. It was a plastic bag. She opened it. It contained two items I'd provided him with: handcuffs and a ball gag.

"Seriously?"

This was too far.

But she didn't mind.

She liked handcuffs, but wasn't sure about the ball gag. She enjoyed being told what to do, being bossed around, being dominated, but this...

She stared at the silhouette. His jerking was getting quicker, more aggressive.

She asked, in the most seductive voice she could manage, "And what do you want me to do with these?"

Ball gag.

143

Now.

She wanted to please him. She wanted him to want her. So she fastened the leather strap around the back of her head and placed the ball in her mouth.

Tighter.

She pulled the strap tighter.

TIGHTER.

She pulled it and it hurt.

His arm moved more vigorously and the grunts grew louder.

And the handcuffs.

She lifted the handcuffs. They were steel. No fluff like those playful handcuffs you find in Ann Summers—no, these were brutal, hard handcuffs, and, for the first time, she became quite unsure. Once these were on, she had no control. She looked ridiculous in the ball gag, but at least she could move. If her husband looked out the window right now, she could run, be out of sight, quickly escape this situation, but once these handcuffs were on, she would rely solely on the man she trusted enough to fuck but not to leave her husband for.

I'm waiting.

She sighed, feeling pressured, just as she did in every other situation in her life; when she was the one who had to pick up the kids; do the vacuuming; make everyone tea; give up her job so her husband could keep his; when she lost her virginity at fourteen; when she had a one-night stand at uni; when she was talked into going back to his house on their first date, just for coffee, just one, just a quick coffee—it's always only a quick coffee.

I SAID I AM WAITING.

She sighed.

Placed the left cuff around her left wrist.

Paused.

She was halfway. She could still walk, or wave, or fight, and she suddenly felt very cold. Her arousal had disguised how cold it was, but it was night-time in winter, and her skin was pricking, goose-pimples were forming, and she was shaking. She wrapped her arms around her body, wanting to cover up its imperfections, and searched for her nightie on the floor.

I SAID I'M FUCKING WAITING

The message made her stiffen.

He'd never spoken to her like that before.

He'd taken charge, plenty of times in fact, but he had always done so with a quiet authority, with a silent confidence that she was to obey and he was to lead. This was different; this wasn't just rough play, this was aggression—something this man had not shown before.

She stared at the figure in the shadows.

Its arm stopped moving. It didn't move. It mirrored her stillness.

The man she was having an affair with was a big, stocky man with a wide frame. This was a thin and scrawny man. Weaker in stature. Hunched over, lacking the same swagger and confidence.

But he had her lover's phone.

She turned her head slowly, her body convulsing in jerks, a mixture of cold and fear, and looked into the glass door to her left, the one that led to the kitchen where she spent most of her evening, and in that glass pane she saw the man's reflection.

She went to scream, but the ball gag muffled her.

She turned, running back toward the house. Her foot had just passed the threshold as she was yanked back, the stranger having grabbed the other half of the handcuff that she had fixed around her single wrist.

She fell, but responded immediately, trying to scramble to her feet. She couldn't. He was holding her down. His face appeared over her. He wasn't frightening like she was expecting. He looked like a boy. No bigger or scarier than her.

He grabbed her hair in his fist and lifted her to her knees. She thrashed her arms at him in chaotic defiance, swiping her nails at his face and punching at his arm. For a moment, she thought he was going to drop her—then he drove her face into the brick wall, just above the outdoor tap.

Her husband often attached a sprinkler to that tap in the summer, and they'd sit in their chairs with a glass of wine and watch their children frolic and play over the jets of water. For now, a large drop of her blood landed on that tap and dripped with a satisfying ooze from the faucet to the paving slab.

TWENTY-SIX

I t was my fault, really.

Brian had taken it too far, and he had never intended to do so. Wanking over her and making her strip off was never in his plan.

It was *mine*.

I made him do it.

It was on a whim.

I felt an impulse, and I went with it.

What can I say? Don't be so shocked! I'm The Devil, you insufferable vagabond—it's my prerogative to meddle and manipulate you dumb fucks into doing inconceivable acts you would otherwise convince yourself you weren't capable of. Exposing your hypocrisy is to me what porn is to you; I get to watch you be defiled, and it spurs me on to do more.

I'd only just let Brian come to his senses and realise what he was doing when she'd turned to run back inside. If she alerted her husband or picked up the phone or, hell, even took off the ball gag so she could scream, he was fucked—he had no choice but to pursue her, grab her by the back of her hair, and ram her head into the wall of the house, forcing her body to drop in a heavy mess onto the frozen grass. It did not kill her, but it was enough to cause a drowsiness that made her easier to deal with.

He watched her for a moment, silent and pensive. It felt like an out-of-body experience, as if he wasn't actually committing these atrocious acts; like blood wasn't trickling down her forehead and into her eye; like she didn't look pathetic with her ball gag in her mouth; like she wasn't naked and humiliated, about to die in disgrace. Under other circumstances, Brian might have considered her sexy, in an older-woman-ageing-naturally kind of way. Now he just found her...

Sad.

Really, truly sad.

He turned away from this wife; this mother; this woman; and he huffed. He didn't want to do this, but the eternity in Hell and the little time he had left to dispose of another three souls held too much prominence in his thoughts, and he knew he had to finish her.

Her eyes were opening, blinking away the blood, and she was starting to come around. He needed to do it quickly.

He just didn't want to.

He looked around the garden, searching for an item that might help him speed up her death. But it was a garden. Leaves and bushes and trees did little in the way of aiding murder.

But there was a pond.

Across the garden, there was a pond.

He peered up at the windows of the adjacent houses. No lights had come on, but that didn't mean that no one had seen him. He needed to do it quickly and get out of there.

He picked up her feet, her skin colder than he was expecting, and dragged her across the grass, leaving a smear of blood behind her. She stretched her arms out and tried digging her fingernails into the ground—but she was too drowsy to put enough strength into it. Still, Brian wasn't that strong, and it took all his might to pull her body across the garden. He stopped for a breather, then did it in bursts; one pull, two pull, three pull, until he arrived at the pond—which turned out to be frozen over.

He sighed. Yet another obstacle. Fate sure wasn't making it easy.

He took the loose handcuff, lifted it above his head, and struck its sharp edge like an ice-pick against the surface. A small crack appeared. He struck it again and the crack grew, then he dragged the handcuffs through it until he created a hole—a rough hole with jagged edges, but enough of a hole that he could punch it and force it to loosen. A few more punches forced it to come free. He dragged her by the hair, ignored her weak protests, and shoved her head underwater.

He held it there.

Her thick hair floated upwards, feeling like eels between his fingers.

He wasn't quite sure how long this would take.

He didn't want to make the same mistake as the last target and leave her alive. At the same time, he wanted to get out of there before a nosy neighbour called the police.

She didn't put up much of a fight, and so he sat there for a few minutes, holding her head under, the water freezing his wrist and hand until they were almost numb.

His gaze wandered around the garden. It was nice. A few benches, trees, a patch of grass for the kids to play football, flowers that would bloom a variety of extravagant colours in the summer. The house was pleasant too—nothing like his, but nice enough for a middle-class family, much like the one he'd grown up in. He wondered what her husband would say when he woke up and found her. Would he be angry when he saw the text messages from another man, or would he be too forlorn to hold a grudge?

Eventually, enough time passed, and her body had long since become still. He freed his hand and took it out of the water. It had turned blue. He placed it beneath his armpit to warm it up.

Her body remained as it was, her buttocks glistening in the moonlit sky, and her head still inside the pond like it was buried in there.

Brian stood. Pulled up his hood. And, with his freezing hand still under his armpit, he left the garden and ran.

CHAPTER
TWENTY-SEVEN

E arly morning light pushed through a haze of clouds, and with dawn came another pang of painful remorse.

Brian kept running.

It was almost time for children to wake up, run into their parent's bedroom, wake their mothers and fathers, and demand to know if Santa had been.

Allison's children would be unaware of what awaited them. Her husband would wake up, turn over, and be confused that Allison wasn't in bed. Perhaps he'd assume that she was making breakfast, checking on the presents, or quietly using the bathroom.

None of them would ever enjoy Christmas again.

The trauma caused by what they were going to see would be incurable. Therapy and Prozac will not fight off the image of their mother's body lying limply on the wet grass, her head stuck in the pond like an ostrich with its head in the ground. It will stay with the children forever, and it will be distorted and made bigger in the way our bad childhood memories are. Their father would not be able to find the words to explain what happened, and would not find any words to comfort them. Their mother died a violent death and was never coming back.

Brian did that to them, and he hated himself for it.

Except it didn't feel like him. He wasn't in control. It was instinct, if that was what you could call it. It wasn't his choice to masturbate, or to torment her before death, or to have her remove her clothes. None of that was his intention, and it felt like he'd been somewhere else, somewhere distant, hovering in the sky over the devastation he was causing, watching as he made the end to this woman's life even more unpleasant.

But he had done it, it was his hands, his text messages, his eyes, his instructions, his actions, and even though he couldn't feel himself in them, he knew it must be him, and it was painful to think, to know that he could hurt a person so much, not just kill them, but to humiliate them, so he did the only thing he could think to do...

Brian kept running.

He wasn't running away as such; he wasn't fleeing or escaping, as the family home he'd left was far away by now. He was running because he had to do something; he had to cure the energy in his legs; the pang in his chest; the conflict raging against the inside of his skull.

He had to run, because every time he thought about what he'd done, the only way to quell the sting was to move.

He was sweaty. Panting. Had a stitch. Muscles aching.

He slowed down to stop at one point, but then it returned, the feel of wet clumps of hair in his fist, the sound of bubbles glugging to the surface of the water, the way her body was suddenly moving and then suddenly... not.

And he kept running.

He pushed himself harder to sprint, sprint, keep sprinting, whatever it took to occupy himself, whatever helped him fight away the sight of the woman suffering before her demise.

The sun had risen, pushing itself halfway up the sky, and he squinted to avoid its glare and turned down a path that would put the sun behind him.

He only had a few hours to finish the last three, and he couldn't waste time—but he couldn't stop running either.

If he stopped, he would have to think about it.

If he stopped, he would see her again.

If he stopped, it would be real.

He turned the corner. And another. And another.

Allison had woken up on Christmas Eve, finished wrapping her presents, fed her kids, texted her lover, and gone to bed with her husband, thinking it was just another Christmas.

She'd woken up yesterday without knowing she was going to...

To...

To...

Brian stopped. Fell to his knees. Screamed. Screamed hard. Until it felt like razors in his throat. Then he screamed even harder.

He was on his knees, but he didn't know how he got there.

He waited for it to rain. Or snow. But it never snowed on Christmas here. It was just cold.

He covered his face. Tried not to cry. Weak boys cried. Pathetic boys cried. Wimps cried.

Then he stopped resisting, and he cried.

And he wiped his eyes, looked up, waited for the kindness of a stranger to comfort him, the hand of an old, wise person to place itself firmly but sweetly upon his shoulder, and for a generous voice to ask if he was okay.

But there was no one around him. He was alone. Completely alone, on a street like any other, on the outskirts of a town, smaller shops nearby, and a larger building directly in front of him. There were a few steps and a wheelchair ramp leading to the entrance. A sign fixed to the ground by two poles read *Sweet Acres Nursing Home.*

As he looked upon the automatic blue doors leading into a blank, sterile corridor, he knew he was in the right place.

DEBT #5 ARTHUR BRADLEY

TWENTY-EIGHT

W hether a person is five, fourteen or 102, humans all have mornings in common—that hesitation to get out of bed; that reminder that you are still alive.

But for Arthur, who had quickly become an old man, mornings were starting to feel tougher.

Not that you ever really age—not in your mind, anyway —and while Arthur's body may be stiff with arthritis, and he may struggle to walk halfway across the room without help, and his breaths may often turn into wheezes and coughs; he did not feel the same in his mind.

And he'd always loved Christmas.

He woke up on Christmas morning in his nineties with the same excitement he had when his age was a single digit. He didn't receive presents from Santa anymore—though he'd received a gift from his nursing home, and one from his grandchildren on their obligatory annual visit—but it had never been about the presents. It was about the feeling. The buzz he only had one day out of 365. And he'd felt it throughout his entire life.

Except, more recently, he'd found that the excitement was starting to die.

His nineties had been... well, different.

That feeling of awe and wonder and magic that rose within him on Christmas morning had turned to a feeling of emptiness; like he was starving, but not for food. For something else. Not love, that was far too melodramatic—but for something to fill the gap that a solitary room in a home of absent minds had taken from him.

He had family. Not his wife, she had perished long ago —but he had sons and daughters, and they had sons and daughters, and they would visit on Christmas like they always did. Except the obligatory visit felt far more obligatory nowadays. His grandchildren seemed nervous with energy, silent with routine politeness, fidgety with an eagerness to return to their new toys. His son's wife would be keen to get on with Christmas dinner, and his son, whilst displaying the most resolute sense of duty out of any of them, didn't ask open questions that might illicit long conversations. He asked closed questions, and he asked them slower and louder, as if Arthur's age made him unable to understand English. His body may be fading, but his mind certainly wasn't.

The nurses were kind. They bathed him, fed him, helped him cross the corridor to mundane activities such as bingo and chess and then more bingo.

They really seemed to like bingo here.

He couldn't stand it. It was a pointless game of luck with an edible prize for the winner. He knew the nursing home was skint, but they could at least offer more than just an extra shortbread with his afternoon cup of tea as an incentive.

Honestly, Arthur was bored, and he wanted to die.

It wasn't an eager wish, nor a craving, it was just a thought, and one he mused on from time to time. He was already dead to his family; they just didn't have their inheritance yet. His existence no longer offered anything to anyone. He did not contribute to the economy, or to the world, or to his loved ones. He made the nurses smile, but it was their jobs to smile, and he struggled to tell what was genuine and what wasn't.

More than anything, he struggled to understand the purpose of going on.

He had lived a long life of love and happiness mixed with conflict and rage. A life where the good times and the bad times passed like phases of the moon, and his mood affected no one but himself. In a few decades, the living generations of his family would die out and anyone who knew him would become a memory that would also soon fade.

He wasn't cynical, just tired. It was hard to know why he was still here.

On this particular Christmas morning, he had woken a few hours before the nurses were due to help him get up, and with a determination to get ready on his own. He managed to pull his trousers halfway up his legs before he gave up. He was too weak to even attempt his shirt. So he just sat there, waiting.

Once, needing another person to dress him might have humiliated him, but these days it was as normal as the birds singing in the morning and the shadows growing at night.

He had earned this.

He had worked all his life for this.

He had saved money for his retirement for this.

And this was how it was. A day filled with absence. A vast space crammed full of nothing.

Once, he had meaning.

Now...

Now he was a burden to those that knew him. Just a body that kept his floral sheets mildly warm. A patient who would be instantly replaced by another after his expiration.

Another Christmas began, and he shook off the feeling.

He was grateful. He'd had a lot. He'd experienced many of life's pleasures. And so he said his prayers and thanked the Lord for it.

Then he sat, and he waited, his trousers half on, for a smiling nurse to come pull them up.

This was what he'd earned.

What a life to be rewarded with.

It only compromised his smile slightly.

TWENTY-NINE

The nursing home felt like school. It had that ominous feeling like you were entering prison in disguise. It was a penitentiary to care for those who society doesn't trust to care for themselves. The corridors were blank, with the occasional poster left over from the Covid pandemic about how to wash hands, and the occasional push trolley with dirty towels on. There was a faint odour, like that which might precede the path to a public toilet with promises of urine-stained toilet seats and wet tiled floors.

Brian hated it here.

He'd hated school. The uniformity of it. The way it felt like living in an oppressive dictatorship. And, since he'd been able to employ a cleaner, he hated uncleanliness, and the stench made him feel queasy. The sooner he could leave this place, the better. After all, this one should be easy—an old man can't fight back, can he?

The only issue was whether he could bring himself to murder his next target. They were old, and near the end—but what if they had done nothing wrong? The last target had hardly been the same level of scumbag as the first—were these becoming tougher? Was this a deliberate ploy by myself?

I cackled over his shoulder at the realisation he'd come to, but when he looked around, I wasn't there. His eyes lingered for a few seconds, vaguely aware of something. He shook it off, pushed open a door, and entered a communal area.

Cheap seats with cheap blue cushions waited around small plastic tables. There weren't many people around them—it was still quite early—but there were a few faces. A man sat at the window looking solemnly outside, his empty expression reflecting years of lonely Christmases and the numbness that accompanies such solitude. Further across the room was an old lady, small, shrivelled and mole-like, veins running up her neck from beneath her dark pink cardigan, and sat opposite her was... Mike? Lily?

What were they doing there?

"Shit," he muttered.

His brother-in-law and niece noticed him before he could retrace his steps back to the corridor. Lily shouted out, "Uncle Brian!" and burst from her seat, sprinting toward him. She threw her arms around his waist and hugged him with such force it made him stagger back.

Mike wasn't so happy. He rolled his eyes and licked his lips like this was typical of Brian, as if showing up at his mother's nursing home was the kind of stupid thing he might do. He said to his mother with a soft voice, "One minute," then trudged toward Brian with his arms folded, the corners of his mouth curved downwards, and his head shaking in the pitiful, begrudging way his head so often shook.

"We're seeing Grandma," Lily told Brian. "Then we're

going home, and we're going to see if Santa's been, and see if he ate the mince pie I put out, and then I get to play with my dolls, and then we're going to have dinner, and—and—are you coming for dinner, Uncle Brian?"

Brian met Mike's eyes. Brian didn't answer.

"What are you doing here, Brian?" Mike asked, his voice glum and blunt in that hostile way that men who work in positions of unearned authority seem to be great at.

"It's a public place, isn't it?" Brian answered.

"But unless you have some grandparent that Clarissa hasn't told me about, I can't think of a reason—"

"I don't have to justify myself to you."

Mike raised his eyebrows and shook himself out of it like he was shrugging off a bad dream. "You're right. I don't give a damn. Come on, Lily."

He held his hand out for Lily, who kept her grip on her uncle.

"I want to see Uncle Brian!"

"Well, you've seen him, now we go see Grandma."

"But I've seen Grandma."

"Lily, come on."

"Is he coming for dinner?"

"Come on."

"But you said he wasn't and–"

"Lily!"

He snapped with such aggression it made Brian's body jolt. It angered Brian with a kind of anger he hadn't experienced much before; this wasn't an irritation by a middle-lane driver, or a dawdler walking in front of him; this was an anger fuelled by love, not by self-justification.

But he stayed calm, caring far more for his niece's happiness than for getting one over her father. Seeing that her eyes were about to tear up, he crouched, turned her toward him, and straightened her jacket.

"You need to go with your dad now, Lily."

"But you're coming over later, right?"

Brian glanced at Mike, whose face was unforgiving.

"Probably not. We'll see what we can do."

"But—"

"I've got things to do. You go to your grandma, she's waiting for you."

Lily smiled. "Happy Christmas, Uncle Brian."

Now it was Brian's turn to fight away tears.

"Happy Christmas. Now go."

Lily nodded and turned to her dad. Mike grabbed her wrist and dragged her across the room until they had returned to his mother's frail body. Mike spoke to his mother without looking back. Lily glanced at her uncle as he backed out of the room and left before the situation could get any more painful.

He walked along the corridor, his mind absent, paying no attention to what was around him. That was, until he came across an open door. The only open door along the corridor.

With a whisper in his ear, I let him know it was the right room.

He paused in the doorway, looking at an old man sat on the edge of the bed in vest and pants, and with his trousers halfway up his legs.

Arthur looked up at Brian with a wounded look; one so vulnerable it was almost impossible to match it to the strong young man he once was.

"Are you here to help me?" Arthur whispered.

"I think so," Brian answered, and entered the room.

THIRTY

B rian sat on the edge of a seat in the far corner of the room. It was too low, and his knees were almost hitting his shoulders, and it felt like the cushion had been worn away. After several seconds of shifting to find a comfortable position that was not forthcoming, he stood, approached a small table that had a plastic tub of organised pills in it, and perched against it. It felt a little wobbly, but he managed to find the right position to keep steady.

Then, finally, he surveyed his next target.

Old, undoubtedly. Senile, not sure. Pathetic, absolutely. His clothes were not fully on, and he was waiting there, stationary, like a lemming, with very little movement. But Brian was still intrigued—why had I chosen this guy?

"Why haven't you gotten dressed?" Brian asked.

Arthur's head lolled to the side, then back again. "Because no one's come to dress me yet."

"Why can't you dress yourself?"

He looked down at the beige trousers around his pale,

veiny ankles. He stretched his arms out, only to find them crack and strain under the fatigue.

"Because I can't."

Brian raised an eyebrow and almost went to continue talking—but didn't. He couldn't stand trying to have a conversation with this man's striped blue and white boxers on show. So he bent over and pulled the man's trousers up for him.

Then something extraordinary happened.

Arthur put his arms around Brian's shoulders, and he held them there, using Brian to support his weight as he raised himself up, thus meaning Brian could lift the trousers until they were around Arthur's frail waist.

This might not seem so extraordinary, but if you are used to being as untouched as Brian, you may understand why the moment was so profound. Not only was it the touch of another human's skin against his—his wrinkly arm against Brian's neck—it was also the reliance. In that moment, Arthur had completely depended on Brian to hold him up. And, as he set the man back down after what was a few brief seconds, Brian couldn't help but feel... well, he wasn't sure what it was. It was odd, though. He imagined it was what some people might refer to as a spiritual moment. For him, it was the first time he'd actually helped a human being that wasn't himself.

And it affected him in a way he couldn't quite understand.

He returned to leaning on the wary table and aimed his gaze at the man. Arthur looked small. Fragile. But I showed more to Brian about this man than he could see with his eyes—I showed him the man's past, the man's present pain, and the man's fatal future. I showed him the wife he loved for sixty years, the child he raised on minimum wage, and the way it all seemed so little to Arthur now. Then I returned Brian to the room, and he could not explain what he knew. He knew he should speak, but the moment had caught him in its grip, and he struggled to release himself from it.

Eventually, he shooed the in-articulable feelings away, dismissing them like his father would dismiss him as a child —he was busy, he didn't have the time, he had things to do.

"Do you know why I'm here?" Brian finally asked.

There was no way Arthur could know this stranger was here to bring about the end of his days. But, with my whisper in his ears, he knew. Somehow, he knew, though he wasn't sure why.

"Yes," Arthur said.

"Are you not going to fight? Or object?"

Arthur set his weary eyes upon the young man. He saw little of himself in the stranger. He had served in the RAF. Was married at twenty-one. With children. He'd remained a committed family man throughout his life, proud to bear the responsibility of providing for his family. But, while they both knew they were different—at least in terms of who they were—there was one thing that could reconcile their differences.

They were both lost.

Arthur shook his head and, with all sincerity, answered, "No. I'm not."

"Why not?"

"When Death is knocking at my door, all I can do is answer."

"That sounds really defeatist."

"That's because I am defeated."

Silence lingered between them. The man elicited only a small amount of sympathy from Brian, but a mass of compassion. He struggled to do what the man was so keen for him to do. He did not want to kill someone who was so lost. At least not until they'd found their way.

"Who are you?" Brian asked, in an accusatory tone he didn't intend.

"I'm Arthur."

"No, I mean—who are you?"

Arthur chuckled. "Just an old man."

"But how..." Brian looked around the room. The pale walls. The monotonous furniture. The stale window displaying a dim sky. "How did you end up here?"

"I got old. It'll happen to you too, someday." Arthur smiled at Brian, then added, "If you're lucky."

"Yeah, but I won't want to end up here."

"Oh, no?"

"I don't mean any offence, but I'll be at home with a wife to take care of me."

"And if she's gone?"

"Kids, then."

"I see. And where is this wife and child now?"

"Well... nowhere."

"And what about the rest of your family? Where are they?"

Brian went to answer and almost choked on the words.

"I thought so," Arthur said. His stillness conveyed a sense of peace. Or maybe it was frailty. Brian couldn't be sure.

"Someday I'll have someone," Brian mumbled, and though he didn't have the confidence to articulate it loudly, Arthur still heard it.

"How will you do that?"

"I don't know. I'll find someone. Someone beautiful. And smart."

"And what will you offer them?"

"Eh?"

"You said you will find someone who will offer you beauty. Intelligence. What will you offer them?"

Brian scowled. This man was being purposefully obtuse. "What the fuck do you mean?" he demanded, feeling his cheeks warm.

Arthur chuckled. "Aggression, huh? Is that what you offer them?"

Brian went to retort, but Arthur cut him off.

"I get it. I understand. That's all I had to offer, once. I didn't find many takers."

Brian looked down. He felt Arthur's eyes on him. He fought away a sense of shame. He didn't let people talk to him like this.

"So what is it you offer?" Arthur prompted.

"Why do I have to justify myself to you?"

"You don't."

"Yeah, well... Don't ask then."

"I can ask all I want. Doesn't mean you are under any obligation to answer."

"Go to Hell."

"I see."

Arthur smiled. Looked to the door. To the sky outside. To the uncomfortable chair that was too low for his visitor. Then back to Brian, whose eyes were still on him.

"Truth is, you don't know what you have to offer, because you've never had to offer anything to anyone but yourself."

"You don't even know me."

"Then tell me I'm wrong."

Arthur received no response.

"I thought so."

Brian shifted position. "Fine, let's turn it around. Why are you so eager to die?"

"For the same reason you're so eager to kill."

"Which is?"

"Because I no longer have anything to offer, so... why the heck not?"

Brian stared at Arthur—not just stared, but *stared*—he penetrated the old man's soul with his eyes, and in doing so, he saw what the man saw in the mirror. Not this wrinkled, dismayed wreck, but a young man who no longer knew who he was. In seeing this, he finally realised why he felt so much for this man.

It was because he'd reached the same precipice Arthur had, but he'd reached it far, far sooner.

"Let's do it," Arthur said. "Before I fall back to sleep again."

Brian stood. "How shall I–"

"I don't give a damn. Just do it."

He looked around. There was no weapon. But there was a pillow.

"Lie down," Brian instructed.

Arthur did as he was told, though he struggled to lift his legs onto the bed. Seeing Arthur's predicament, Brian lifted them for him and placed them carefully on the dim white sheets.

Arthur smiled up at him, his arms crossed over his chest like he was already in his coffin.

"I'll try to make it quick," Brian said.

"My boy, you make it whatever you need it to be."

Brian took the pillow, lifted it over Arthur's head, and stepped toward him.

Arthur closed his eyes.

Then Brian paused, intrigued by his final thought.

"What would you do?" Brian asked.

"Eh?"

"If you were me. How would you be better?"

Arthur smiled at Brian like he'd finally asked the question he was waiting for all along.

"Find something you love more than yourself," Arthur said. He took a deep breath, then added, "And hold on to it."

Arthur relaxed. Widened his smile. And waited.

Brian put the pillow over the old man's head and held it there until it was done.

DEBT #6 CHARLES BUFFET

THIRTY-ONE

He walked without stopping—out of the old people's home, down the street, and through the fresh dawn of Christmas. It was light, and a cold humidity hung in the air that would make the average person freeze—but Brian, in his short-sleeved t-shirt, felt none of it. Dried sweat clung to his clothes like it possessed him, and he refused to let himself think.

He just walked.

He was even paler than he was before. Even bonier. Even grimmer.

I had destroyed this boy's entire sense of being, and I loved it—I relished it—I yearned for it. Honestly, you met him at the beginning of the story—didn't he deserve to be brought down a peg or two?

He viewed everything in his life as it affected him, saw all events with the black and white view of *For Me* and *For Someone Else*. And now there were all these other categories coming up, other layers of life he hadn't thought possible, people who weren't just things that got in the way, complexities that meant that this world wasn't just filled with obstacles—but that it was filled with people who were as scared as he was.

Any other day he would have dismissed Arthur as an annoyance—but there were no annoyances anymore. Only people who fought their own self-resentment through any means necessary, just like him.

And so I took the opportunity to destroy him.

To show him who he really was.

To let him see what he'd never seen before—to observe just what a bastard he'd become.

He covered his eyes; he covered his ears; but it could not conceal his memories, and he dug his fingers into his head, hard, harder, as he bore witness to every deluge of pain he'd ever contributed to; every moment where he'd chosen malice over empathy; every incident where he'd made someone's life worse when he could have so easily made it better. I showed them all at once, making them constant, making him feel his regret, tormenting him with remorse; he witnessed all the mental agony he now resented himself for creating; every nasty word he'd ever uttered and every tear at the end of it.

That boy he abused online for being bad at Call of Duty was an insecure teenager, covered in pimples, crying at night because he didn't fit in.

That elderly woman who dawdled in his way in the exit of the supermarket, prompting Brian to bump her aside, justifying it to himself by saying that she was waiting on death's door anyway—that woman had lost her husband and barely saw her children who were too busy living their lives. Her interaction with Brian was the only interaction she'd had with another human being that week.

That woman he'd sent nasty messages to because she accused his favourite rockstar of molesting her before withdrawing her accusation—she wasn't lying, she was just fed up; fed up of the abuse, of her sexual past being interrogated, of her fetishes being exposed, of being re-traumatised through every reference to the hideous night—so much so that she said she was lying just to make it stop. She was a human being, and Brian was bursting with a new awareness he wished he'd had before.

That person he'd abused online for having a different political view; that kid he'd called fat; that old man in the nursing home who'd been forgotten—they all suddenly became people.

And they all deserved better.

All the things he'd done, said, shouted, posted, messaged; all the shit he'd given Mike; all the shit he'd given his parents; all the shit he'd given everyone—he had never considered that they were humans with as many faults as he had.

Until now, he'd been faultless. Indestructible.

And now he was the worst man alive.

He paused on a bridge as the last memory passed. Pulled at his hair. Sunk to his knees. Stood again. Screamed into the river below. Turned away from a man passing him with a bag full of presents. Punched the brick wall and grabbed his fist.

So many feelings ran through him and he couldn't recognise a single one, couldn't pick out a word to describe it, couldn't access the vocabulary required to articulate what he was experiencing.

He screamed again.

And he fell to his knees.

And, keeping his hand over his face, he leant against the side of the bridge and sobbed.

Sobbed, sobbed, sobbed.

Like a little bitch.

And he didn't stop until he heard me sniggering.

He took his hands away. Looked up. Saw me and my wide smirk. Saw the satisfaction this was giving me. Saw that this was what I'd intended all along. Saw that no amount of physical torture could equal the mental servitude of knowing you've lived your entire life wrong.

"Fuck you," he muttered.

I sniggered more. His face curled up. Oh, the rage. I fed off it. Breathed it in. He thought it was good to show how much he hated me, but it was exactly what gave me power. Without this kind of rage, I would never be here. Without this kind of rage, I wouldn't have already won.

"What now?" Brian said, his voice marred by the ugly contortions of his weeping. "Who are you going to have me kill now? Two more, is it? Who are they?"

I raised my eyebrows. "Are you ready to know?"

He scowled at me again. I saw defiance in him. I thrashed my red, pointed tail against the side of the bridge to remind him who I was, shooting a spark of fire across the surface. His resolve disappeared and his onslaught of despair continued.

"Quit crying," I told him. "You are so weak."

He went to object, but didn't. He wiped his tears. Didn't bother getting up. He seemed to prefer it at my feet.

"You don't have long," I told him. "Are you ready?"

A happy couple walked past, laughing. Their smiles faded as they saw Brian in his dishevelled state. They averted their eyes and hurried on, just as most people would.

They didn't so much as divert their gaze in my direction.

"Why didn't they—" Brian went to ask.

"They can't see me."

"Then how can I?"

"Because I let you."

"What if you're not even real?"

"Wouldn't that be a kicker? You've imagined me this entire time, and have just been killing for no reason. Man, that would be even better..."

"Maybe I stop believing in you. Maybe I think you're just in my head."

"Maybe you shut the fuck up and stop being so fucking stupid."

He sighed. Turned away. There was that spite returning, that fury. Oh, humans are ever so predictable.

"Arthur was a nice old man," Brian said. "A nice old man and you made me kill him."

"It was what he wanted, wasn't it?"

"Yes – but that could have changed. I could have helped him. Could have visited him."

"Could you?"

"Yes!"

"And if you'd have seen him yesterday, moseying on down the street, getting in your way, would you have helped him?"

He looked down. He got my point.

"So who is it next?" he asked. "Some hero? Another parent? Mother Teresa?"

"You know where to go."

Of course he did. I'd given him the information half an hour ago.

"The soup kitchen?"

"Yes."

"Oh, what, you're going to have me kill some homeless guy?"

"No."

"What, some charity do-gooder working there?"

I smile.

"Oh, come on!"

He threw his hands in the air and looked away.

"You know the alternative, don't you?" I said. "Don't kill him. Enjoy your Christmas morning, then at midday you come with me."

"I can't kill someone like... Like that..."

"But if they were homeless, you'd have been fine with it?"

He went to speak, but didn't. Instead, he used the wall of the bridge to pull himself to his feet.

"Are you ready to say no to me, Brian? Are you ready to sacrifice yourself to eternal torment so a good man can live?"

"What if this is all bullshit? What if it's a test? Yeah—what if the aim *is* to get me to sacrifice myself, show that I'm a good person, show that I would do that? Then I will pass the test and get to live. Maybe that's what you're doing—and by killing these people, I'm condemning myself anyway."

"You think too much."

"Well? Is that it?"

"Brian, there is no deeper purpose. I just want to watch the world burn."

He looked down, ran his hands over his face, through his greasy hair, and shook his head. I stepped forward and whispered in his ear with tangible delight, "But you can always say no and find out."

He lifted his head to the sky. Closed his eyes. Wished he was somewhere else. But there was nowhere else.

Eventually, he turned to me and said, "Show me the way."

I grinned and led the way, walking beneath the hazy sky toward the clarity of death.

THIRTY-TWO

We watched from the doorway. Men with caps and hats and beards and tattered denim jackets and blankets around their shoulders and wrinkles on young faces and filthy combat trousers and weary eyes all lined up, their feebleness apparent, their melancholy prominent, their lack of meaning stark.

It is quite common for a human to sneer at such a sight; to turn their noses up and walk away. But I bet you pretend you don't. That you're better. That you regard the dregs of society with respect. But you all have an elevated sense of self-worth that reality finds to be quite unrealistic. Let's be honest, when you see a disaster on the news, you tut and you shake your head, then you get on with your life; when you hear a nasty comment, you walk on and don't get involved; and when you see a homeless soul against the street corner, you give space between you and them, avoid eye contact, and do everything you can do to avoid seeing what your glorious capitalism has done to those who don't succeed.

You judge everyone but yourself.

So whilst you are inclined to look down on Brian for his preconceptions about the homeless population, and whilst I am indeed hesitant to defend this sordid wretch, you are deluded if you think you are any different.

Charles, however, *is* different.

He is the exception.

Charles would never scoff, or turn his eyes away, or dismiss a weary fellow on the street. He'd give them his change, or buy them tea, or find them an umbrella. His compassion for his fellow man extended far beyond any other human's.

And, true to his character, he was spending his Christmas morning serving food in the homeless shelter.

He scooped the ladle into the soup, poured a generous portion into a bowl, and smiled at the homeless fellow as he handed him the bowl. His smiles remained determined and undeterred despite the misery that gazed back at him. He was one of those infuriating people who were happy all the time, and I couldn't imagine being able to tolerate much of his company.

Brian checked his watch. He had a little over an hour until midday. His time was running out. But he was torn. This one was different. This wasn't a paedophile or a murderer or a druggie—this was an honourable, well-intentioned man. A man who was better than most. A man who helped others even when there was no reward.

He was the man you often pretend to be, but for Charles, it was not a façade—he was a true altruist.

"Well?" I prompted.

"I don't know if I can do this."

"Then what are you doing here? I'd use this hour to say your goodbyes—we'll be going as soon as the bell strikes twelve."

He dropped his head. Sighed. Closed his eyes. I saw the turmoil bubbling within. He knew he had to do this. And as much as he fought it, I knew he was going to do what was best for himself.

We all do.

Without another look back at me, he walked forward and, in a very British way, joined the queue—as if he should be polite before he murders a man.

He's pathetic. You all are.

Soon enough, he reached the front, and Charles poured a bowl of soup and offered it to Brian, who looked at it with guilt—he felt he shouldn't take it. He didn't deserve it.

"I'm not homeless," he grunted.

Charles' smile did not falter. "I won't tell if you don't."

Brian exhaled and briefly closed his eyes. How was he meant to kill this man?

Charles handed the bowl to the next man in the queue, wiped his hands on his apron, and looked at Brian with a misinformed warmth and generosity.

"Are you okay?" Charles asked.

"I..." Brian looked up. Into the eyes of the man he had to kill. He couldn't say anything.

Charles turned to someone behind him and shouted, "Janine, cover me!" Then he turned to Brian and nodded toward a fire exit behind him. "Come on," he said. "I need a cigarette."

Brian, looking back to see if I was there, followed on. Charles placed a hand on his new friend's shoulder as he guided him out of the fire exit and into an alleyway.

The alley was dark. Full of shadows. Overflowing bins lined the wall. Overnight rain dripped from the gutters above. There was a smashed window to a basement at ankle level, and Brian couldn't help but scan the shards of glass that stuck out from it, each of them sharp and able to pierce a throat.

He turned his head away and sighed again.

Charles took out a cigarette. Menthol, mint flavoured.

"You want one?" he asked.

Brian shrugged.

Charles put two in his mouth and lit them both. He handed one to Brian, who took it warily between his forefinger and middle finger, then stared at it like it was dirty.

Charles took a long drag, relished it, then exhaled a puff of smoke.

"Gosh darn it, that's good," he declared. "My wife hates them, so I rarely get to smoke anymore. Gave up years ago, but every now and then, I get a chance, and boy is it good."

Brian stared at Charles, mouth open, his thoughts frozen, unable to fathom the situation.

"So," Charles said as he leant against the wall and took another drag. "Why don't you tell me what's troubling you?"

Brian tensed. "Why do you think something's troubling me?"

"You're not homeless and you're in a homeless shelter. You look like you've been dragged through a gutter. And you have an expression like someone has done something terrible to you. You don't have to tell me, I know I'm a stranger—but perhaps a stranger is what you need. So, I'll ask again, why don't you tell me what's troubling you?"

Brian's eyes fixed on the cigarette. Smoke rose from its perfect end. He placed it between his lips, took an inward drag, and the end lit up amber as the cigarette shortened. He pushed out a puff of smoke. Charles was right, it was a good cigarette.

"Told you, didn't I?" Charles said.

Brian couldn't help but chuckle, even if he still didn't smile.

Charles reached out his arm, placed his fingers beneath Brian's chin, and lifted his face to force eye contact.

"What happened?" Charles asked with such charm there was no way Brian couldn't answer it.

"I... I have to do some things... I mean, I've done some things..."

"Bad things?"

Brian nodded.

"We've all done bad things, my friend."

Brian scowled. He doubted this man had done a bad thing in his life.

"But that doesn't make us bad people," Charles continued. "Good and bad just isn't that simple."

Brian considered this. "I... I've hurt people..."

"So have we all."

"I mean, really hurt people... I... I had no choice."

"How do you know you had no choice?"

"Because... Because I had to..."

"If you had to, then what's upsetting you about it?"

Brian gazed into the eyes of this man, wishing his father had been this caring. He could not bring himself to kill him. He couldn't. And he almost made the decision that he wasn't going to.

Then a glance at Charles's watch urged him to hurry.

"I just... I..."

"You didn't have a choice."

"Yes... I didn't..."

"My friend, we all have a choice. All of us."

"But I didn't."

"And what makes you so sure?"

Brian went to reply. He didn't know. Because he did have a choice. Hell or murder. And he'd made his choice.

And as he made the choice not to hurt this man, he felt me over his shoulder, lingering behind him, grinning intently at the back of his head.

Brian turned over his shoulder and looked at me. He resembled a weak wreck of a man. Even more than he had been at the beginning of the night. I loved it.

"I can't do it," he told me.

"Do what?" Charles asked.

"I can't," Brian repeated, not looking back at Charles, focussing on me.

"My friend?"

"Please... I can't hurt this man..."

"Hurt this man? Who are you talking to?"

Charles stopped leaning against the wall, took a step forward, and peered down the alleyway behind me. He was clueless. No idea what was there, behind Brian, whispering in his ear.

As far as he was concerned, Brian was talking to nothing.

"I won't do it. You can take me to Hell."

"To Hell?"

Brian looked back at Charles. Stared at him. The smart demeanour, kind face, welcoming eyes, soft hands, soothing voice—he could not bring himself to do this.

"I can't kill you," Brian whispered.

Charles's smile finally faded.

Brian turned and begun his stride down the alleyway.

"What does that mean?"

Charles pursued Brian—

"My friend?"

—sped up, trying to catch him—

"Please, talk to me?"

—reached his hand out to turn the stranger around—

"Let me help—"

—and he slipped.

His foot slid through the mud of a nearby puddle. His feet rose above his head, and he fell backwards.

His neck landed on a shard of glass in the broken window.

And I laughed.

Oh, how I laughed.

Hard. Loud. Until my guffaws echoed around the alleyway.

Brian stopped walking. Glared at me. And turned back to Charles.

Charles, who laid on the soggy, filthy ground, his throat impaled, blood trickling down his smart shirt and squirting across the wet walls, his eyes widening and closing, suffocating, weakening, desperate.

This was the face of a man who knew he was about to die.

Brian fell to his knees and put pressure on the wound. It just made things worse. The shard was still lodged in Charles's neck, and the pressure on the wound just shoved the glass in further. Thicker, longer squirts of blood fired across the alleyway like a broken tap, spraying the walls with this man's demise.

Brian wanted to do something, but he had no idea what do to. He couldn't lift the man for fear of making it worse. He couldn't put pressure on the wound to stop the bleeding. He couldn't perform CPR as the man's mouth was full of blood and his windpipe had been skewered.

So Brian did the only thing he could think to do.

He held Charles's hand.

And he brushed Charles's hair off his face. Wiped the blood from his eyes. Tried to give him the same reassuring smile Charles had given him.

And he stayed by the man's side through the last desperate, suffocating breaths he took. As the realisation of death spurred more fear in Charles's eyes, Brian spoke to him gently, telling him it would be okay, telling him there was a Heaven; not because he believed it, but because he knew it would help the man to believe it.

And if there was a Heaven, this man was surely on his way there.

As the last glugs and dribbles of blood ended, the grip on Brian's hand loosened, and Charles's eyes emptied. His body fell limp, and the sixth target lay dead on the filthy ground, disgraced in death by an accident in a soggy, sordid alleyway.

It was time for the final target.

THIRTY-THREE

B rian trudged out of the alley, wiping tears from his eyes, and he glared at me with all the hate he could muster, destroyed and dejected, battered and beaten.

He gave me exactly what I wanted, and I fed off it.

"They are hunting you, you know," I told him.

"What?"

"The police. They've found the bodies and they think it's a spree killer. They are checking CCTV as we speak. You need to get to the final target before they get to you."

He shook his head. Looked back over his shoulder into the alleyway. Charles's open eyes stared back, sparkling in the reflection of a streetlamp. If you didn't know what those two small dots of light were, you could easily mistake them for a cat's eyes, hiding in the shadows and searching for its prey.

"You did that," he said. "Didn't you?"

It was more a statement than a question. I replied with a grin.

"You really are a bastard," he said.

"You forget who I am."

"Fuck you."

I chuckled. "You have one more target, and you have little over forty minutes to complete it."

Brian turned away from me. Covered his face. Leant against the wall.

"Tick tock, Brian."

"Just, shut up – just give me a minute!"

"You don't have a minute."

"I said shut up!"

I stretched out my arm and clenched my fist. Brian bawled over in pain, grabbing his chest, screaming from the agony, punching the wall to relieve it.

I unclenched my fist and the pain stopped.

He scowled at me.

"You ought not to forget who I am and what I can do," I told him.

Brian looked away. Looked up. To the sky. Shook his head. As if he was pleading with the Heavens. Then he turned back to me. Threw his arms in the air.

"Fine! So where am I going now? A children's hospital? The orphanage?"

"You know where you need to go."

I let him feel it.

See it.

Let the anguish of it sink in.

And I watched as his humiliation was complete, as the realisation fell over him, and he understood what he'd been building up to this entire time.

"Oh, no," he said. "No, no."

"Oh, yes."

"No!"

He saw it again.

Felt it.

Knew where he was going.

It was only a short walk. Around the corner. He'd been there before. Many times. When he was welcome.

He wasn't anymore.

"No. There's no way. No."

He backed away from me.

"Come on," I said. "Let's walk together."

Brian shook his head, refused, backing away further, gesticulating his arms in defiance.

So I showed him the alternative.

And he saw it. Pits of fire. Lava running through his body instead of blood. Claws impaling him in all the nasty places. An eternity of this beautiful torment.

And he stopped backing away.

"Now."

He wiped his eyes and hobbled to my side. We walked down the street together, as if we were equals.

We could never be equals.

Nevertheless, reluctantly, he walked on.

This next part is going to be delicious.

DEBT #7 LILY

193

THIRTY-FOUR

The house sits before him like an old friend he has since betrayed. It's the same pristine lawn, the same white picket face, the same arrogant front door—but it's different. It's the pathway to doom. An ominous line of slabs driving him toward fate.

He stands at its end, staring, looking it up and down, scanning each window and each brick and dreading it all the while.

Meanwhile, his fancy watch ticks on, less than twenty minutes until midday.

Why couldn't it be Mike he had to terminate?

No, even then he'd struggle. As much as he despises the guy, he's a good dad, and he wouldn't want to force Lily to grow up without him.

His posture drops. I watch him give up, resign himself to Hell, give in to the eternal torture. So I prick his skin with a reminder. Force a projection into his mind, like a cinema screen displaying fire and lava and claws, screams in surround sound, wails and screeches battering the inside of his skull, until he's crouched with his hands over his ears shaking his head, whimpering no, no, no, no, no.

"Then do it," I tell him.

"I can't."

"You don't have a choice."

"I... I just can't."

"She'll be in Heaven forever. She'll be happy. In a better place. It's an easy decision, really."

I want to see how much I can push him. How far he will go. How close he will get to cutting his niece's throat.

I love doing horrible things to horrible men.

"Get up, Brian."

He rises, slowly ascending, hunched over, his greasy hair over his sweaty face, his arms weak and heavy.

"I'll be with the all the way," I whisper.

"Will they see you? Will they know why?"

"Only you will know why, Brian. Only you."

He checks his watch.

Fifteen minutes.

He hobbles forward, his body weary, aching, fatigue of a stressful night filling his legs with led, a stab of pain on each step toward the gallows, like wading through water with razors in his skin.

He reaches the front door. Knocks on it. The noise makes him flinch. Steps come from inside. The door opens.

There he stands.

Mike.

His face a painting of disgust.

"What, Brian?" he spits. "What are you doing here?"

"I..."

Brian looks up at a man who is so much better than him. Smartly dressed, hair swept to the side, upper middle-class smugness smacked across his face.

In this moment, Brian realises why he hates this man so much.

It's because he envies him.

It's because Mike is everything Brian's opportunities should have led him to become, but instead Mike is everything he is not.

"I thought we made our feelings clear," Brian says. "I thought we'd told you to—"

"Uncle Brian!"

And there is the voice.

The shining light among the darkness.

The beckoning finger toward absolution.

The innocent against the wretched.

She appears at Mike's side, and Mike clutches her arm to stop her getting any closer to Brian, like her uncle is an animal escaped from a cage and he's warning her not to get too close.

"Are you coming in, Uncle Brian?" she asks, youthful optimism sticking to her voice.

"I…"

"No," Mike says. "He isn't. He was just passing. Weren't you?"

Mike gives Brian the eyes.

Brian ignores them. Gazes at the girl who means so much; the girl who means life; the girl who means death.

"Are you not coming in, Uncle Brian?"

"No," Mike says. "He's not."

With Brian void of words, Mike goes to shut the door, but Brian shoves his foot in the way and halts it. It shakes the wood. Mike looks furious. Brian hates him more right now than he ever has.

"Yes," Brian says. "I've come to see you. I'm just popping in."

"Yay!"

Finally, she unleashes herself from her father's tight grip and bursts outside, shoving her arms around her uncle, and squeezing him with no idea what the world has in store for her.

"Do you want to see what Santa brought me?" she asks, her voice quick, full of fever, full of excitement. "Do you want to? It's so awesome!"

Brian looks behind him.

Our eyes meet.

I nod.

Twelve minutes.

I'll be with you all the way.

Brian looks down. Looks back at me. Then returns his gaze to the house.

"I'd love to," he says, and Lily drags him inside by the hand.

THIRTY-FIVE

T he living room looks like a cheesy Christmas card —the large Christmas tree in the corner decorated with colour coordinated tinsel and baubles; the large array of opened presents with a bin bag in the corner full of wrapping paper; the warmth of the heating in complete ignorance to the cost of living; the smell of roast turkey and steamed vegetables wafting in from the kitchen; the well-dressed, neatly groomed family giving each other love in way that seems too genuine.

Lily drags Brian into the living room by the hand and pulls him to the floor. She sits cross legged and Brian perches on his knees, surrounded by colouring books and puzzle books and crayons and books about things only children would find funny. She shows him boxes of dolls, houses, cars, doll hair brushes, and many other accessories that will be forgotten by New Year, but today seem like the best thing ever.

It reminds Brian of Christmases when he was a child. When he'd have everything. It was always an expectation, not a privilege.

"Brian?" Clarissa's voice startles him. She stands in the doorway, wiping her hands on her apron, taking a break from cooking in a scene of misogynistic bliss.

Mike stands beside her. His arms folded. His sneer unhidden. His stance the epitome of manliness.

"Hi," Brian says.

"Mummy, look, Uncle Brian came, he's come to see my presents, I'm showing them to him!"

"That's lovely," Clarissa says to her daughter, then turns back to Brian. "Why are you here?"

Why is he here?

Good question.

He turns to the clock on the fireplace.

Six minutes.

He looks at Lily.

She never stops smiling. She's the only person who cares whether Brian is here, the only person in the world who loves him unconditionally—and he's got to send her to Heaven to avoid going to Hell.

"I thought we made it clear what we thought about you being here," Mike says, his voice so stern and flat that it draws Lily's attention.

"What's wrong?" she asks. "Don't you want Uncle Brain here?"

"Lily, go help your mother in the kitchen."

"No! I want to stay with Uncle Brian!"

"Now."

She goes to stand, but finds Brian's hand around her wrist. He doesn't realise he's holding her, but he is.

"Let go of her," Mike says.

Brian shakes his head.

"Who the hell do you think you are?" Mike bends over, jabbing his long finger at Brian, his face a painful grimace.

"What are you going to do, Mike?" Brian says. "Hit me?"

"Don't hit him!" Lily says. "Why would you hit him?"

"I said to go help your mother."

"She's not going anywhere." Brian keeps his grip on her wrist. She winces from its tightness, but doesn't attempt to shake him off.

"Why don't we all calm down?" Clarissa says.

Her proposition doesn't calm anyone down, but it does bring forth a stubborn silence – the kind of silence that lingers too long, that implies weakness of the person who breaks it, that does nothing to quell the tension.

Mike rolls up his sleeves. His toxic masculinity surfaces. He doesn't want to kick Brian's arse in front of his daughter, but he seems to be considering it.

Brian glances at the clock. Five minutes.

"Brian–"

"Shut up, Mike."

"How dare–"

"I was in this family long before you were."

"Yes, and what a legacy you've left." Mike advances on Brian, another stride and another jab of his finger with every statement. "Disappointment to your parents. Unable to love your sister. No real job. Lucky without deserving it. Pathetic in every way."

Mike stands over Brian, his finger inches from Brian's face.

Brian considers the things he's done in the past 24 hours. The things he now knows he's capable of. His eyes scan Mike's throat, and he considers what would happen if he slit it. Whether Clarissa would forgive him. Whether he could claim self-defence. Whether he would be seen as the aggressor when eliminating this cretin from the world. Just imagine all those people who work under him, who hate him as a boss, who would be so much happier without a narcissist like this micromanaging them.

He would be doing the world a favour. He was convinced of it.

He glances at the clock. Three minutes.

He looks down at Lily. Her eyes are wide. Her body is shaking. He didn't realise he was still gripping her wrist. He releases it.

Even so, she doesn't leave. Doesn't do as she's told. She remains loyal by his side.

"Honestly, Brian—what would the world be missing without you in it?"

Brian goes to retaliate, but doesn't. Honestly, he doesn't disagree with him. He's been a leach. He's not a good brother. Or uncle. Or person. He deserves Hell, in a way.

But he has a task to do.

And Mike will never understand what is about to happen.

"Fuck you, Mike," Brian says. "You were never good enough for my sister."

Brian glances at Clarissa, standing in the doorway, looking like a housewife from the fifties, weak and weary, unwilling to stop her husband's aggression, unable to find the strength to stand up to him.

Then again, she never stood up to Brian either.

The clock. Two minutes.

"I don't have a knife," Brian tells me.

"What?" Mike retorts, but the statement was not for him.

"I don't have anything I can use."

"Yes, you do," I whisper in Brian's ear.

Brian looks down. There, in his open palm, is the leather

handle. The blade is sharp. Lethal. One jab in the throat and this will all be over.

"Let's take this home," I tell him. "It's time to end this."

Do it, I tell him.

He stares at his niece.

Flexes his fingers around the leather handle.

Do it now.

It's time to see how far I can really push him.

THIRTY-SIX

K *ill her.*
    I'm in his ear.
    I'm shouting in whispers.
I'm saying what he needs to hear.
Just a little encouragement, that's all.
He's come this far.
He's done this much.
Just one little swing. One little touch.
You are so close to ending this Brian, so close.
Kill her.
I'm over his shoulder.
I'm by his side.
I'm looking up at him from the floor.
I'm glaring down at him from the ceiling.
Kill her.
I'm screaming.
I'm sighing.
I'm murmuring.
I'm gesticulating.
Kill her.

He looks up.

Mike sees the knife. He cries out, demands to know what he's doing, why he has a knife, why he is standing over his daughter, why is he doing this, why is he here, why oh why oh why oh why oh why are these mortal imbeciles never able to see past their own self-aggrandization.

He swings an arm to stop Brian but Brian swings one back and the knife slashes across Mike's chest and Mike collapses and clutches his chest and he tries to stop Brian again because it's his daughter after all and he clambers forward and Brian swings and this time its deeper and he's choking and blood is soaking his top and he's on his knees not moving any closer

just pleading

from the floor

an arm outstretched

please don't hurt my daughter

please don't hurt her

please.

Kill her.

Clarissa's hands are over her mouth

she doesn't move

she is too feeble

their parents raised her to be a subservient woman

they raised her exactly as they intended

Kill her.

Mike reaches an arm out with an open fist and with a calm voice like he's negotiating a company merger and he asks nicely so nicely please he says please it's your niece you love her you don't want to hurt her you don't want to do anything just put the knife down you can be part of our family I understand I was wrong but please just please just please put the knife down

Kill her.

Lily doesn't move.

She looks up.

Despite her feeble expression, she's the toughest one here.

The only one who is defiant in the face of what must happen

and brian lifts his arm in the air

i don't want to

he says it over and over

i don't want to i don't want to i don't want to

please don't make me

please

Kill her.

He locks eyes with me and he sees nothing but blackness, nothing but red, nothing but evil, nothing but hatred, nothing but nothing but nothing but nothing.

There are more of me.

We stand all around him.

He can't see anything beyond me.

On the walls. The ceiling. The floor. The window.

In Mike's face.

In Clarissa's face.

In his reflection.

But not in Lily's face.

Oh, not in Lily's face.

Never there.

One minute.

Kill her.

he whimpers

begs again

please don't make me do this

and the begs turn into shouting and he tries to drown me out

Kill her.

NO

Kill her.

DON'T MAKE ME

Kill her.

PLEASE STOP

Kill her.

I DON'T WANT TO HURT HER I DON'T WANT TO HURT HER I DON'T WANT TO HURT HER

Kill her, Brian. I am tired of waiting.

sirens outside.

they have come for him.

his spree has been noticed and there's plenty of CCTV and I'm surprised they have taken this long

they figured he would be here

they came in their droves

the sirens are wailing

they are outside the house

they are here Brian

they are here

Kill her.

NO

Kill her.

STOP IT

Kill her.

I DON'T WANT TO KILL HER I DON'T WANT TO KILL HER WHY DOES IT HAVE TO BE HER WHY

thirty seconds

Lily's hand reaches up.

Not a defiant act, or an aggressive act, or a nasty act.

A compassionate one.

One where her soft skin meets his course, cracked knuckles.

And she strokes his hand.

Her young, soft skin touches his.

He has never been touched before

not really

not properly

not lovingly

but here, in the face of her death, a child with the empathy of a million noble humanitarians, empathy even her parents can't manage, lets him know it's okay.

That she's here.

That she loves him.

Twenty seconds.

Kill her.

he's crying now

tears

streaming

cheeks wet

red

ugly

Kill her.

Sirens outside. They are here. They are going to take him away.

I CAN'T

Kill her.

I CAN'T

Kill her.

I CAN'T

Yet still he holds the knife.

Still he holds it high.

Still he clutches it with all of his life.

His sister and brother-in-law are silent now.

It is only Brian, Lily, and myself.

The only ones he's aware of.

And I surround him and I push him and I tell him it's time, it's time, it's time.

Kill her.

LEAVE ME ALONE

Kill her.

PLEASE

Kill her I CAN'T DO IT *Kill her* NO I WILL NOT *Kill her* LET ME GO *Kill her* NOT HER NOT HER NOT HER NOT HER *Kill her* NEVER *Kill her*

The door bursts open. There is shouting.

ten seconds

They tell him to get to the ground.

he looks up at lily's throat

She looks down at him.

Kill her.

And he looks at me.

Into my eyes.

Deep, into my mythical eyes.

A creature he never believed in in the first place.

And he says, quietly, and calmly, No.

He drops the knife.

They tackle him to the ground. His wrists are bound behind his back. There's a knee in his spine and it's uncomfortable.

Lily keeps her hand on his shoulder throughout the entire ordeal.

And, as he is dragged to his feet, and he looks around for me, he finds that I am not there.

That I have never been there.

That there is not a single sign of me in this home.

The police talk. We have him. You are under arrest on

suspicion of murder. You do not have to say anything. If you do not mention. Anything you do say.

He doesn't listen.

He watches his niece's eyes.

And she watches back.

Until the very last moment.

Until he is taken from the house.

Until he will never see her ever again.

HELL

THIRTY-SEVEN

The floor and walls are arranged in one metre by one metre squares, each one a different cushion of the padded cell. They are sterile white – the kind of white that screams cleanliness whilst mocking purity. The only thing that isn't cushioned is the ceiling. Oh, and Brian's head. But it doesn't matter, because his head can't meet the ceiling, and the walls cushion his manic stampedes against them.

Besides, with his arms tied so securely around him in a straitjacket, any time he tries to run at the wall he just loses balance and topples over anyway.

You see, Brian's mind is not here anymore.

He isn't even sure he's still alive.

But he is alive.

Oh, he is very alive all right.

Honestly, I wasn't entirely sure that padded cells like this still existed. If it was a Victorian mental institute where they sent the deranged and hysterical, fine, but not here. Not in today's world. Not like this.

But it turns out that they do, and oh, it is so very satisfying to witness!

Eventually, Brian's frenzy ends, and his energy runs out. His fever will return soon, and he will once again bounce from wall to wall, satisfying me with his indefatigable torment—but for now, his morning's dose of pills has finally kicked in, and he is docile. Sitting in the corner. Bags under his eyes. Hair in clumps of grease. Rocking back and forth, ever so slowly, as if someone has nudged him and now he can't stop swinging like a pendulum.

Back and forth.

Back and forth.

Back and forth.

He wants to see me again.

Not because he likes me.

None of you ever actually admit that you like me.

Despite most of your revolting actions being more akin to my approval than your pathetic deity's, you still never admit how important I am to your existence.

He just wants answers.

He isn't entirely sure what happened on that Christmas Eve night all that time ago...

How long ago was it, exactly?

A month?

A year?

A decade?

Hell, he could have been in this psychiatric unit for centuries.

He's been sedated for most of it. He just wouldn't stay still. Wouldn't stop shouting. Wouldn't stop screaming. It was the only way the nurses could handle him.

He's been declared unfit for trial. Not in a fit mental state to face prosecution. A decision considered by the public to be abominable—they want blood—they want justice—but they haven't seen what a nutcase he is. For now, he is confined to these walls indefinitely. And you know what indefinitely means when it comes to situations such as this, don't you?

It means *forever*.

And even his sister doesn't visit him.

In fact, her life has improved a lot without him there. Her husband was promoted to CEO of whatever bullshit business he's in, thriving on the power of white privilege and subtle chauvinism. With his new pay cheque they've been able to move to somewhere much, much better and much, much farther away.

Lily has entered her teenage years and become interested in boys and phones and has forgotten all about the pathetic uncle she once adored when she saw the world through a child's eyes.

And still, he lives, he remains, he continues.

For nothing, and for no one.

Just for the sake of it, really.

No point. No meaning. No purpose.

Just breathes, in and out. His heart beats, slowly because of the drugs. His head twitches occasionally, and the nurses often wonder if there's anybody in there.

Take him off the drugs and you might find out.

It is one random day, many years after the Christmas incident—nothing special about it, a day like any other, with the sun rising and setting as this wretched man remains in a padded cell with no windows—that I make my final appearance.

Final for Brian, anyway.

He's rocking. Muttering, but nothing intelligible. Having

conversations, mostly in his head, sometimes aloud, but with no one to respond.

He feels like he's being watched.

And he looks up.

And there I am.

Out of focus.

Whether this is my intention or the effect of his drugs, it isn't clear to him, but it doesn't need to be.

He looks inquisitive. Turns his head to the side. Squints. Unsure whether he is seeing what he's seeing.

I step toward him, slowly, each placement of my foot purposeful and pronounced, until I am standing over him and he is staring up at the underside of my chin.

"You... It's... You..."

They are watching on CCTV. It's the most coherent his speech has been in a long time, and once they notice, they can't look away. Oh, how intently they watch the screens, gripped by intrigue, hushing each other until they are silent, listening carefully to what Brian has to say.

"You... Did... This..."

I did nothing, and I make sure he knows it.

"But... I... You..."

I crouch over him and run my claw down his cheek, past his stubble, and flick the overgrown hair off his neck.

He asks me the only questions he wants to ask, and he asks it so clearly that one might almost think he is cured.

"Are you even real?"

I emit a grave, low chuckle, sinister and clear. I lean over him, let him see my grin, and I say, "That is the question people have been asking for thousands of years."

And I stand.

And I back away.

And I fade into nothing.

And he stands and he charges the wall and he screams and he shoves himself back and forth, cursing at me with all the vigour he can, and the nurses come rushing in and hold him down whilst a doctor with a nice, big needle comes along and sticks it in his neck.

That is the last time Brian ever sees me.

I leave him be and move onto the next abhorrent human that deserves my attention.

There is a whole world of delusional dregs willing to believe in incredulous nonsense waiting for me.

And I am their puppet master.

And I am moving onto the next fool.

Speaking of which, hello there, Reader – nice to meet you. How would you like unending wealth and success?

I promise, you won't have to do much for it.

Not yet, at least.

Not yet.

JOIN RICK WOOD'S READER'S GROUP...

And get three eBooks for free

Join at **www.rickwoodwriter.com/sign-up**

HAVE YOU READ ALL THE BLOOD SPLATTER BOOKS?

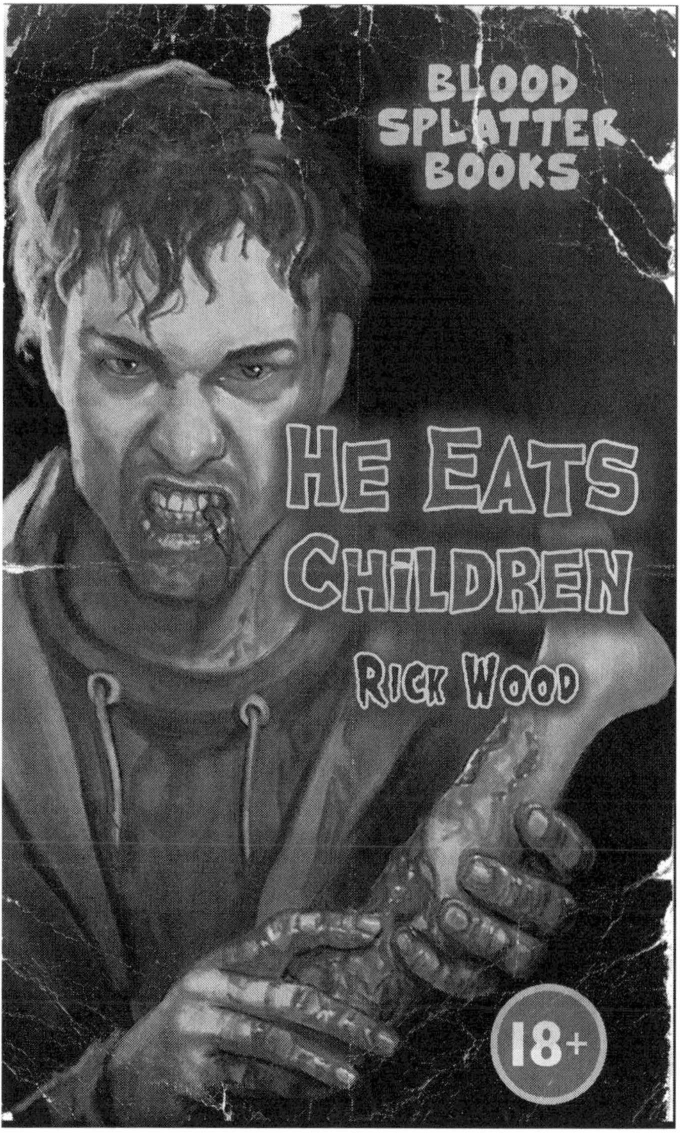
BLOOD SPLATTER BOOKS
HE EATS CHILDREN
RICK WOOD
18+

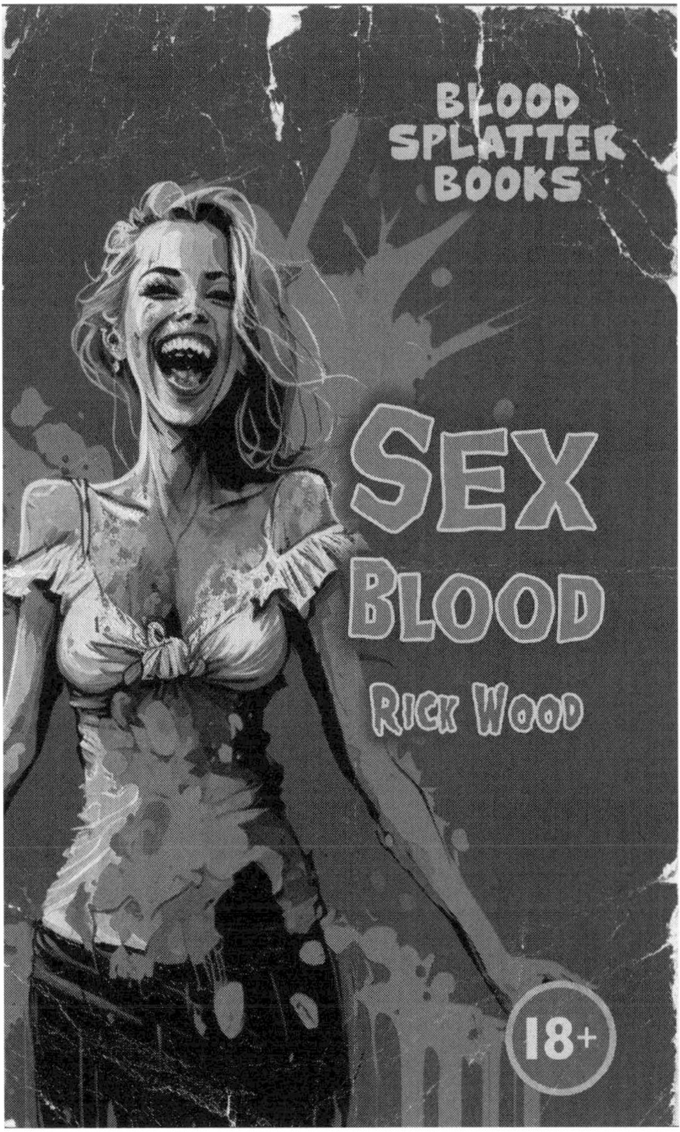
BLOOD SPLATTER BOOKS
SEX BLOOD
RICK WOOD
18+

BLOOD
SPLATTER
BOOKS

This Book
is Full of
BODIES

Rick Wood

18+

BLOOD SPLATTER BOOKS

WOMAN SCORNED

RICK WOOD

18+

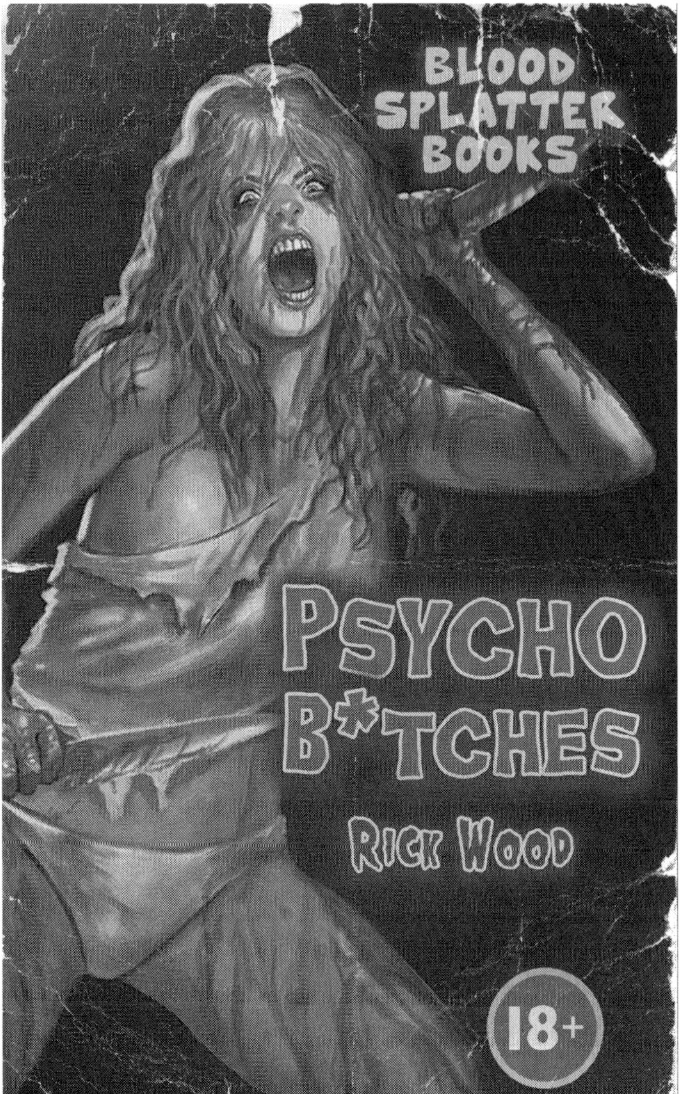
BLOOD SPLATTER BOOKS
PSYCHO B*TCHES
RICK WOOD
18+

BLOOD SPLATTER BOOKS

HAUNTED HOUSE

Rick Wood

18+

BLOOD
SPLATTER
BOOKS

HOME
INVASION

RICK WOOD

18+

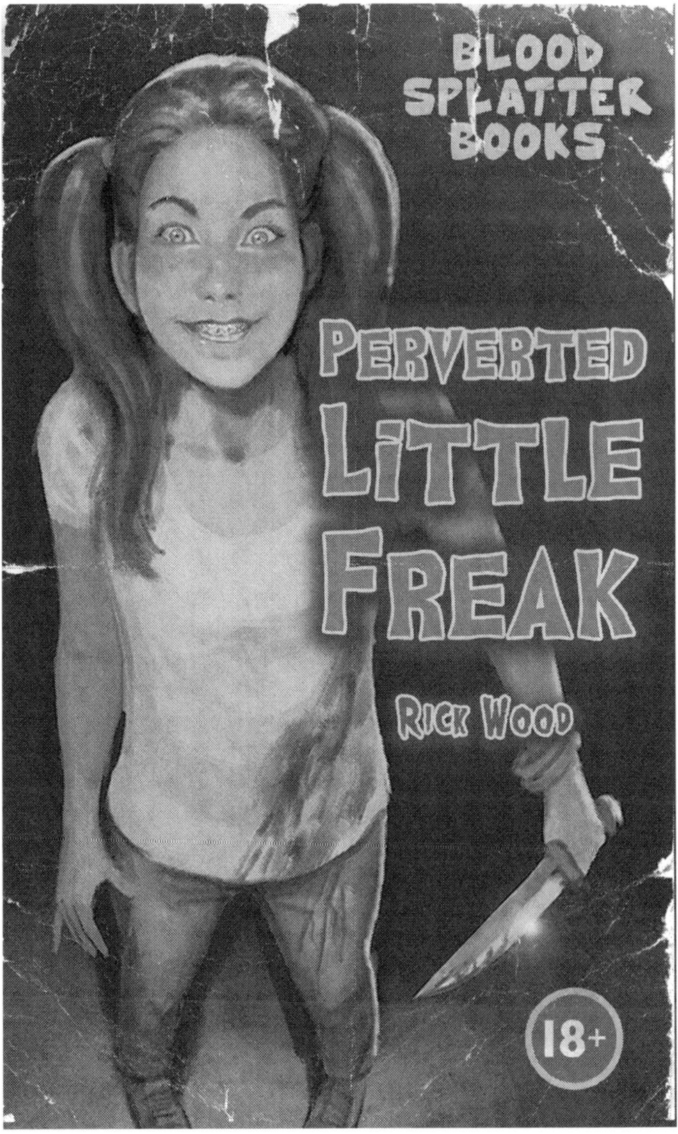
BLOOD SPLATTER BOOKS
PERVERTED LITTLE FREAK
RICK WOOD
18+

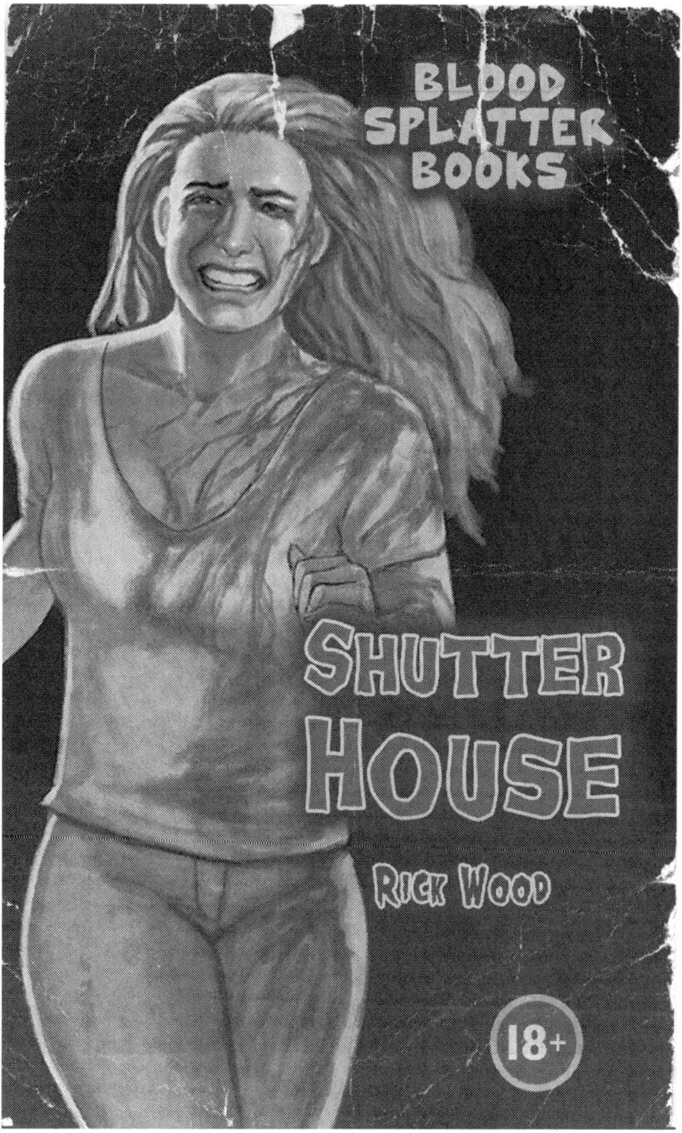
BLOOD
SPLATTER
BOOKS
SHUTTER
HOUSE
RICK WOOD
18+

Printed in Great Britain
by Amazon

31526734R00142